# Visions of Redemption

Mr. Costales' account of the adventures of Bove Sandle is captivating. "Visions of Redemption" caught and held my interest so tightly that I stayed up until 2:00 last night to finish it. His characters are drawn just right, the dialogue is realistic, and the space technology is convincing. I easily visualized the futuristic environment as I read. But the best attribute of the story is the plot presentation. The pace kept me anxious to see the next page and the suspenseful unfolding events were thoroughly engaging. I was on the edge of my seat.

--- Dion C.

An interesting journey, this one. A little slow at first, hang on it picks up speed. Solid characters with good rapore

---. Tina

Great beginning to a hopefully longer series. Excellent storytelling from a great imagination.

-- naumad

Loved the story!

--- Jon

Also by Jon H. Costales

Visions of Redemption

# The Adventures of Bove Sandle

## Visions of Deception

By Jon H. Costales

The Adventures of Bove Sandle
Visions of Deception

First edition January 2024

ISBN: 979-8-8691-0982-8
White Dog Publishing

For my children and their children

# One

At the edge of the Phoenix-Gamma system space rippled and boiled as if the temperature had risen, and elemental particles pulled together forming protons and neutrons then atoms and molecules which combined into structures creating a Kazon scout ship fully formed and functional. Seth, the pilot, dazed and confused, released a breath after the succession of the pain, a side effect of the entanglement transit.

He started the engines setting the velocity to one-thirty-second light-speed and vectoring towards the fourth planet Kryth near the outer rim of the Kazon empire. It was situated technically outside the empire's control, but because the Kazons are wary of others they check nearby systems regularly, hence the scout mission. Seth, a cat-like creature, expected to find nothing unusual during this routine surveillance mission. He ran a paw over his head fur laying his ears back and yawning.

After switching on autopilot, he retired to the sleeping bay to rest. It would take six days to reach Kryth, so relaxation would occupy him for the duration. *Another routine information-gathering mission,* he thought and yawned.

As the ship approached the fourth planet an alert beeped to tell him the location. He cut the speed to thirty-five thousand kilometers per hour to establish an orbit around Kryth. Once stable, Seth gazed down at the great blue ball below as he switched on various monitors, to photograph, record sounds, test air, check the weather, etcetera. Lush green forests of enormous trees that rose three hundred meters from the forest floor covered three-fourths of the land masses while grassland and deserts covered the rest. The oceans made up two-thirds of the planet.

Seth was to be in orbit for two weeks before heading to his next destination. Again, little to do while the ship recorded its findings. But a brief time after the monitoring started, a soft beep alerted him to an abnormality. He slid into his seat and checked the display to discover a settlement among the tall trees. It was a moderate size of two to three thousand inhabitants. *This is not right;* he tapped a pad with his extended claw to increase the magnification for more detail. This planet was supposed to be uninhabited and not scheduled for colonization.

The display zoomed in on the settlement showing people walking through the streets, into and out of buildings. Some lingered speaking to one another before continuing about their business. The ship recorded every detail while running comparisons of all known species. A message flashed on the display identifying the species as human. Seth stared at the information for a couple of seconds in disbelief. *This can't be*, his claws extended and tapped the arms of his seat. "Check for other colonies," he ordered the ship.

Two days later he compiled a message to the Kazon home world describing his finding of a human settlement on the fourth planet of the Phoenix-Gamma system. He pressed *send* knowing something was not right.

*            *            *

Bove Sandle dozed on his bunk aboard the Ibex waiting for clearance to land. The trip from the edge of the Sol system took six days and the crew was anxious for some free time. Those days were exhausting and Bove was having trouble keeping his eyes open. Sleep pushed at his mind demanding he relent and soon he found himself giving way to peaceful slumber.

He felt a hand touch his shoulder pulling him wake. Slowly he opened his eyes expecting one of the crew to tell him they had received permission to land, but instead, before him stood Kabluff watching him as he realized the truth. "What?" Bove said, still half asleep.

"Yes," Kabluff said, "we must talk. Many things have happened, and you are needed once again."

Bove shook his head trying to clear it, "No, these visions are over! This can't be!" He sat up, ran a hand through his hair, and looked around.

Kabluff watched him for a moment then said, "Do you remember your commitments? Your redemption? You must honor what you have committed to, and you must do it now."

"What? I've done everything you asked."

"Yes, you did, but that's only a beginning. Your redemption is not complete until we are satisfied that you are truly committed to continue to do as we ask."

"What?" Bove had committed to stop acts that may harm someone. He had committed to keeping people safe, to protect them by doing the right thing. Not to do what Kabluff asked. "I didn't commit to do your bidding."

Kabluff raised a hand stopping Bove, "We only ask that you do the right thing. The thing that is best for everyone, including you humans."

Bove took a breath and looked around, he was in a small room with a couch on which he lay, a chair, and a small table. There was a single window that looked out at a field of grass and flowers. "Where am I?" he asked.

"It doesn't matter," Kabluff said. "Your colony on Kryth has been discovered by the Kazons."

"Who are the Kazons?"

"They rule a section of the galaxy near Cetus which is close to Phoenix-Gamma and Kryth. And they are very touchy about anyone coming close to their territory."

"What does that have to do with me?"

"You, Bove, must intercede with the Kazons and the humans to avoid conflict. You failed to stop the colonization and now since the Kazons have discovered your colony they will not let it remain."

"How do you know what they'll do?" This was like all the other visions, Kabluff telling him what to do whether he agreed or not. But in the end, they would get their way because Kabluff saw it as Bove's commitment, and then there was the bog. They say it is to help everyone, but still, who are they to impose their will on him?

"Experience," Kabluff said. "No more needs to be said. This situation will quickly escalate if someone doesn't step in to stop it. And that someone must be you."

"No, I have no authority to speak for my government, and I'm sure the Kazons won't listen to me. No, you need to find someone else, someone more qualified than me."

"The Kazons will make an issue of this, no doubt. They have in the past over smaller things. They consider Kryth within their territory, or at least close enough that it should be theirs. They will do something, and your colonists will be in danger. You must consider this." Kabluff said then added, "There is the bog to keep in mind as an alternative." And with that, he waved his hand in front of Bove's face.

Bove woke with a start when he heard a soft knock on his door. He shook his head trying to clear the vision from his mind and said, "Enter."

Jack stepped into the cabin, "We received clearance to land."

"Good, I'll see you on the bridge."

Jack left and Bove stretched and shook his head again wondering about the vision and how important it might be, but he couldn't give it much thought, there were more important things right now.

*        *        *

Unknown to Sharia, the human colony on Kryth, another city, Valcina, existed on the far side of the planet and was shifted back in time such that anyone living in the present was unaware of it. Valcina was the home of the Krytheans left to guard the Sovaka mines, where crystals grow that allow their time-arresting machines to work. They mine the crystals and ship them to the new planets in the far sectors of the galaxy. The machines can stop time in selected locations for months while other locations are unaffected. The technology is simple, but the crystals found in the Sovaka mines are needed to make it work, so the mines are a sacred place the Krytheans wish to remain unknown.

Since the founding of the human colony, the mines had been in peril, and now that the Kazons discovered the colony there was more danger. Steps to stop the colonization had failed and a move to keep a conflict from occurring between the humans and the Kazons was started.

The council chamber in Valcina is the seat of the *troika* and is a vast open space surrounded by tiers of seating rising to the dome high above the central dais. Eight thick columns carved with animals support the dome which was covered with a mural of clouds and birds. The walls of the chamber have scenes of tall forests, huge mountains, and vast oceans. In the emptiness of the chamber the voices of the *troika* echo from the walls and ceiling for no one to hear.

"As you know," Hex said, "a Kazon scout discovered the human colony and reported it to his home world. And from experience, they will make a claim that will end in conflict. Because of that, I have instructed Kabluff to use his resource to stop any conflict before it comes to that."

"Is that the best approach?" Calix asked. "His resource failed to stop the colonization."

"I agree," Ezra put in her opinion. "His resource is weak and ineffective."

"His resource, Bove Sandle, has shown resilience and is the only one available," Hex said.

"But still, he failed. Had he succeeded we would not be in this situation." Calix pointed out.

"Yes," agreed Ezra.

"As I said," Hex narrowed his eyes and his voice lowered, "he is the only resource available, and we will use him."

"It should be determined with a vote," Calix said.

"Very well," Hex replied, "but first we will speak to Kabluff." He turned to his assistant. "Bring Kabluff."

The assistant hurried off and quickly returned with Kabluff who took a seat in front of the *troika*, folded his hands in his lap, and waited.

"Your resource," Hex began, "failed his first mission." He let that statement sit in the air for a moment. Kabluff waited, it was common knowledge that Bove had failed to stop the colonization, so why bring it up? "Some of us," Hex continued, "are not sure he's capable of completing this mission."

"He was very successful with his second mission," Kabluff said.

"That is of no consequence. If the Kazons and humans engage in conflict we will be in the middle, so your resource must be successful. You understand?" A statement more than a question, Hex took a breath waiting for Kabluff to respond.

"Yes," Kabluff said. "I have seen what he is capable of when under pressure."

"We believe the Kazons will want the colony removed," Hex said. "We want the same but without conflict. So, can your resource stop a human and Kazon conflict?"

"I'm sure he can," Kabluff assured Hex.

"Very good," Hex said. "You may go."

Kabluff nodded and left.

Hex turned to Calix and Ezra, "It is done. The resource has been activated."

"That was not your decision. You have overstepped." Calix scowled at Hex.

Ezra nodded agreeably.

"So be it," Hex said waving his hand in dismissal.

# Two

Bove looked out the window of the AutoCab at the run-down buildings--peeling paint, broken windows, trash on the sidewalk and in the streets. The West Village in New Brunswick was the worst part of town. "Are you sure about this guy? Can he finish the work?" He asked Dan, who was the ship's expert. "Is he reliable?"

"Yeah," Dan said, "Take the next left." The AutoCab slowed to make the turn. "Stop at three-ten."

The paint on the building at 310 was not peeling but the windows had a steel mesh hiding the window displays. The metal door opened easily as Bove and Dan walked into a dim interior crowded with shelves of Mech Drones—QRs and AZs, stealth hoods, a couple of Ion Cores, microfoam filaments, containers of dark matter, light motors, and almost anything else a starship would need. The quantity of equipment stunned Bove, and he continued to browse while Dan stepped to the counter and tapped the bell sending a soft chime through the store.

"Yeah, in a second," a voice came from the back room.

"Bee, it's Dan."

"Dan who?"

"Jones."

"Hey, hey, Danny boy," B-Rich stepped out of the back room. He stood almost six feet with a square face, thick brown hair, and a glint in his eyes. "What are you doing in this part of town?" He looked Dan up and down, then turned to Bove, "And who's this?"

"We have a job for you," Dan said. "And this is Bove, a friend."

"Yeah?"

"Yeah." Dan grabbed Bove's arm and pulled him to the counter. "We have a starship that needs upgrading. You interested?"

"What's it need?"

"A little of everything. Bove can explain what he wants."

B-Rich turned to Bove who explained the need for an upgraded transit drive, long-range sensors, life-support backup equipment, upgraded computer systems to run everything, and weapons all around the ship—front, back, both sides, top, and bottom. While Bove explained B-Rich made notes.

"That's not cheap," B-Rich said.

"How much?"

"Half a million, or so. I need to see the ship." He leaned against the counter looking at Bove, "You got enough credits to cover that?"

Bove nodded "Yeah, not a problem."

*      *      *

The next day B-Rich came to the spaceport, looked over the Ibex, and then agreed to do the upgrades. They would have to move the ship to his maintenance facility outside of town and it would take six to eight weeks to complete the work.

Bove told the crew the plan for the upgrades and said they would need to occupy themselves until the work was done. No one complained and welcomed the time off. Being cooped up in a starship for weeks at a time was stressful and everyone needed a break. They agreed to meet back at B-Rich's maintenance facility in seven weeks.

Bove moved the ship there that afternoon and took an AutoCab back into the city, where he rented an office. It had an auxiliary room where he could set up a cot to sleep allowing him to save on renting a hotel room. The other room would be an office where he would interview candidates for the pilot position, which was vacated when the former captain, Lucus, was shot and killed. The crew voted Bove as captain when he stopped Lucus from turning over Stella Throne to Zabidiah "Zabi" Rice, an arms dealer. Bove's move to captain left the ship without a pilot, so Bove selected five candidates for the job and scheduled them for a talk. Ryan Shorter was the third and as he settled into a chair, Bove looked over his resume.

"Why are you looking for work?" Bove had checked the background of each candidate and knew their history, but he wanted to hear it from them. Anyone willing to lie to get ahead was not someone Bove wanted on his ship.

"I had a falling out with my former employer," Ryan said, "more of a difference of opinion—and I couldn't continue working for him." He shifted in his seat uncomfortably and looked like he wanted to say more but hesitated.

"Couldn't or wouldn't?"

He clenched his fingers around the chair's arm, then relaxed them. He had been a pilot for the last ten years and was able to fly almost anything, including starships. Not only was he a good pilot, but he had experience as a medic that he picked up during his time in the military. He used it in a couple of revolutions they were involved in--not his choice--but when the captain decided to take part in a conflict, Ryan went along. So, he learned to deal with conflict and injuries when they occurred. "There were practices that I did--do not--agree with, and I refuse to take part in them. So, I couldn't, and wouldn't, continue to contribute."

"Exactly what did you disagree with?"

Once again Ryan tensed, eyes glancing from side to side to avoid Bove's. He lowered his head looking at his feet as if deciding what to say next. Then he looked up and cleared his throat, "They were dealing weapons to anyone that would pay with no consideration for what they were being used for. I couldn't continue to be part of that."

"Well, we don't deal in weapons."

"What do you do?" Ryan sat straighter in his chair, his hands relaxed, and a smile played on his lips.

"We have medical equipment and supplies. We trade in other goods. Sometimes we take a special assignment to help someone in need. Would you be okay with that?"

"As long as your dealings are legal, I could live with that," he said and scratched the side of his head.

"Your medical experience will be a plus. Tell me about that." Bove studied Ryan while he pondered his response.

Ryan nodded and glanced to the left and then to the right, "I was military for several years as a medic then used my training in a couple of revolutions we were involved in." He looked around the small office, "Where's your ship?" he asked, changing the subject.

"It's having some enhancements installed. Improvements to make things easier for the crew." Bove noticed the change of subject and directed Ryan back to what he wanted to know, "So what revolutions were you involved in?"

"Nothing very serious. There were a couple of minor uprisings that needed our help to put down. They were settled quickly with few casualties." Ryan gave Bove a smile that didn't reach his eyes.

"When did they start dealing in weapons?"

"During the time we were involved in the revolutions, I left shortly after I found out about it."

"Okay," Bove felt all right with that. Ryan seemed to be telling everything about his dislike of his former position. "How big were the crews on your ships?'

"There were twenty-five including me." Ryan pushed his chair back and moved a little to get more comfortable. "How many are in your crew?" He asked.

"Five."

Ryan shook his head, "That's different. And you need a pilot and a medic?"

"Yes, our former pilot has other responsibilities that prevent him from piloting. As for the medic, we travel all over the galaxy and have been in some dangerous situations where someone could be badly hurt. If that happened, we could lose them, but medical training on board could avert that."

Ryan shifted in his seat, pulled at his collar, and took a deep breath. "Yeah, I see what you mean," he said. "So, I guess that responsibility would be mine?"

"Yeah," Bove paused letting Ryan think about that, then he continued, "Does the job sound interesting? Something you would like to try?"

Ryan looked down and shook his head, then ran his hand across his forehead, as if to clear sweat from his brow, and looked up at Bove. "Yeah, I'll try it. But if I don't fit in or whatever, how long before we return here?'

"Can't say. We have a lot of cargo, and we may pick up more. It could be months before we return. Is that going to be a problem?"

Ryan didn't meet Bove's eyes, but looked past him briefly then said, "No, it'll be okay." Then before Bove could say anything Ryan continued, "You didn't tell me what the pay is."

"What's your expectation?"

"A hundred thousand a year," Ryan said.

"We work differently than that." Bove hoped Ryan would be acceptable to being paid from profits. He took a breath and continued. "No one makes a salary or has a regular paycheck. We split the profits from our trading and sales."

"Oh," Ryan looked perturbed, shook his head, and asked, "How does that work?"

"We're all owners of the ship and, as owners, everyone has input in what we do. For example, during our last trip, we were involved in a rescue and retrieving some weapons. As a result of that, each member of the crew received a hundred thousand credits. When we leave this time, all profits will be split among the crew. Is that acceptable to you?"

"You said you didn't deal in weapons.'

"That's right. The weapons belonged to the person we rescued, and we took her and the weapons to her home world."

"Oh," Ryan paused. "So, you didn't buy them…"

"Right, we only delivered them."

Ryan thought for a moment, shifted in his chair, and then asked, "You said everyone is paid a share of the profits and everyone is part owner of the ship. How will that work for me? And how do I become part owner of the ship? That is if I stay."

"Good question," Bove answered. "I'll give you an advance on profits, five hundred credits. That will last until we make some sales. As for ownership, I will have to give part of your share to the crew until you've earned an equal amount. But I'll have to write out the details."

"Do you expect to sell your cargo?"

"We do and we will get more along the way."

"Things have been slim. I haven't been able to find any other positions. I can try this for this trip, but if the income isn't sufficient, I may look elsewhere. Is that okay?"

"That's fine. So, you're taking the job?" Bove crossed his fingers hoping for a *yes*. Ryan was the best candidate he had seen, and the remaining two resumes didn't look as good and had no medical experience.

"Well, I guess so," he didn't sound too sure and shook his head again.

"Good," Bove felt the tension ease from his shoulders. "We leave in five to seven weeks. You can contact me in five weeks for an update on departure."

"Okay."

"Good, see you then."

Bove ushered Ryan out of the office, feeling he would handle himself in a touchy situation with his experience and involvement in the revolutions from his prior position. *Yeah, he'll be fine*, Bove assured himself.

# Three

Arnold Pencaster, the military advisor to the president, sat opposite the expansive windows lining the east side of the room. He laid a folder in front of himself on the eight-foot mahogany table. Against the side wall under a clock sat a small bureau with a coffeemaker, sugar, creamers, and cups. Landscape pictures adored the opposite wall, and behind him, whiteboards covered the wall that separated the conference room from the rest of the administrative building.

Pencaster looked out the windows at the expanse of deciduous trees that made up the view. He tapped his folder on the table and looked at the four men included in the meeting. They watched as he opened the folder and retrieved a single page then laid it on the table.

"What is this about?" James Richerson, the Deputy of foreign affairs asked.

"It's about our national security," Pencaster said.

"How so?" Richerson looked around the table assessing the mood of the others.

"We have received a communication from the Kazons claiming that the Kryth belongs to them."

"What the hell?" Beauregard "Beau" Butler – Four Star General of the space force—stood up, turned around, and gazed out the window as his hands curled into fists, "Where the hell do they get off saying they control a planet we started colonizing six months ago?" He turned toward Pencaster.

"Calm down, Bo." Pencaster extended his hand toward the chair, gently guiding him back into his seat. "We'll figure this out."

"The Kazons?" asked Senator Robert Buchanan. "Who are they?"

Beau tapped his fingers on the tabletop and looked at the senator, "They're in a section of the galaxy towards the constellation Cetus," he said stepping to the whiteboard and beginning to draw. "We've had some contact with them in the past, but that was a while ago." He made an oval on the board and then divided it into fours. "This," he said pointing to the lower left section, "is our area, and this," he pointed to the upper right sector, "is the Kazon Empire. Excuse my drawing, the Kazons control a smaller area than we do. At least they did a few years ago."

"Cetus?" Buchanan asked. "Isn't that near one of the rogue colonies we founded some years back? Like a hundred and twenty years ago?"

"A hundred and fifty years," Peter Wills, Buchanan's assistant, said. "It's one of a couple of hundred colonies we established at that time. We sent hundreds of ships to colonize worlds but left them on their own. So, they are not too friendly to us. But…"

"That's enough history lesson for now." Pencaster interrupted. "We need to figure out what to do about their claim."

Richerson shook his head. "It's not right."

"No, it's not," Pencaster agreed, "But let's look at this in a logical manner. First, we need to get as much information as we can about them and their territory. We currently know little. When we know more, we can determine if they actually have a claim, and decide what needs to be done. Does that make sense?"

Richerson glared at Pencaster, shook his head, and started to say something, but Pencaster raised a hand, palm out facing Richerson, and said, "We need to get more information, right?"

Richerson paused and slid his chair back from the table. "Yeah, I guess so," he conceded.

"What, exactly, did the message say?" Buchanan asked.

"It's from a Tyco Rill, the Military Advisor to their high council. He copied the head of their council and a few other Kazons," Pencaster said.

"Other Kazons?" asked Butler.

"Yeah, I don't know them. Other members of their council and advisors. I guess all the people that need to know what's going on."

"Okay," Buchanan interrupted, "What was in the message?"

Pencaster picked up the sheet of paper he had lying in front of him. "So," he said, "the message is from the Kazon high council and addressed to the Human Ruling Class with the subject of, *In reference to the occupation of Kryth*. Pencaster paused. "The message says, 'Members of the Human ruling class it has been noted that a Human colony has been established on the planet of Kryth. As you should be aware, Kryth is within the territory of the Kazon empire. Because you, Humans, have violated our territory the colonists must be removed immediately. We will do whatever is necessary to ensure the sovereignty of our planet and our empire.' And it's signed by Tyco Rill." Pencaster laid the message on the table.

"*Whatever is necessary*, what does that mean?" Buchanan asked.

"It sounds like they will move them if we don't," Pencaster said.

"Or remove them," Butler added.

Everybody turned toward Butler concern clear on their faces. The room fell silent. Pencaster touching the document sighed.

"They didn't give a time frame," Buchanan said.

"They did say *immediately*," Pencaster pointed out.

"For them to do *whatever is necessary*, they didn't give a time frame for that," Buchanan responded. "They must realize we can't move anyone immediately. Maybe they want us to make plans *immediately*. Or tell them *immediately* we'll do something." Buchanan said, "So, I don't see the urgency to move anyone. In fact, I don't think we need to worry. Let them stew about it."

"To be on the safe side I will prepare an invasion force." Butler said, "Better be ready if they decide to press the issue."

"Does the colony have any protection?" Pencaster asked.

"A police force," Butler said.

"Put a division there. That should deter any immediate action."

Butler nodded.

"What do we have close to Kryth? Say within ten light years?" Pencaster asked.

"Not much," Butler turned back to the whiteboard, erased it, and drew a new picture. "This," he said pointing to a circle on the left of his new drawing, "is Kryth, and this," he pointed to another circle, "is Edonia. It's twelve light years from Kryth. And eight light years from Vakomi, a Kazon base."

"Do we have people on it?"

"Yeah, six cities with populations in the hundreds of thousands. It's well established."

"Good. Base your fleet there and wait for further word."

"That's one of the original colonies. Are they friendly to us?" Richerson asked.

"They haven't been hostile," Butler said, "but we haven't interacted with them in several years. I believe they will be receptive to a base when I explain the situation."

"Very good," Pencaster said. "So," he continued, "we'll have protection close to Kryth, and we'll gather more information about these Kazons. Agreed?"

Everyone nodded in agreement.

"We must make sure they understand that Kryth is ours," Richerson added.

"I agree," Pencaster nodded to everyone. "I will speak to the president for his input."

The meeting broke up among murmuring from everyone.

*      *      *

Carlson Frederick Wilson sat behind his mahogany desk as Pencaster lay a paper in front of him, "What's this?" he asked.

"That," Pencaster said, "is the report on Kryth. The Kazon Empire claims it is within their territory."

"The Kazon Empire? Who the hell are they?"

"A faction in a different section of the galaxy. They want to make a name for themselves by claiming they control the space around Phoenix-Gamma. We've had limited dealings with them in the past, but nothing recently."

"What are they asking for?"

"They want us to leave."

"Well, tell them we're staying. Kryth is our newest colony. People are living there, a couple of thousand as I understand. And we are not going to leave. Tell them that."

"It's not that simple, sir. As the document states, they are willing to defend the planet in the interest of their national security."

"Their national security? How do they figure our colony threatens their security? We're light-years from them."

"You're right, but they don't see it that way."

Wilson leaned back in his chair, arms crossed over his chest, "What do you recommend?"

"We need more information about them and their capabilities. In the meantime, we should respond and give them the impression we are considering their proposal." Pencaster shifted in his chair and leaned forward looking Wilson in the eye, "We don't want this to escalate."

"You think it will?" Wilson asked standing and turning toward the picture window behind his desk. "Are we prepared if it does?"

"I have Butler on standby in case. I told him to beef up Edonia, a planet twelve light years from Kryth. It's our nearest colony and has six cities."

"What's their next move?" Wilson asked, turning back towards Pencaster.

"We don't know enough about them to guess. We need more information."

"I suppose you have a plan, don't tell me. We can do an information-gathering mission as long as we don't stir up any trouble. We are already facing issues with some of the colonies. People think we're so determined to expand that we're not doing the required research before going ahead. This will feed right into their narrative, and it could blow up in our faces if it gets out." Wilson leaned on the back of his chair, "I don't want any issues with our colonization, do you understand?"

Pencaster nodded.

"This is my legacy, my mark in history." Wilson stepped around his chair closer to Pencaster, "Make sure this stays under wraps, understood?"

"Yes, sir," Pencaster said. "I'll plan a mission, something low-key, inconspicuous."

"Good. Then get rid of them, or at least get them out of our sector." Wilson sat down indicating it was time for Pencaster to leave.

Pencaster acknowledged the gesture. "Will do," He stood up. "Will that be all?" He asked wondering how he was going to get a mission together without alerting anyone.

# Four

Bove was concerned about the crew, which he hardly knew, and being captain for only a few weeks left him wondering about loyalty. There was Tom who backed Lucus until Bove had put him in his place with a punch to the solar plexus. He had been loyal since then, but was he just biding his time to get back at Bove? He was the main issue confronting Bove and the command of the ship. If he proved to be loyal and not a threat to Bove's duties as captain, then things would work, but if not, well, Bove would have to face that when the time came.

And Dan, who was Tom's friend, was he loyal to Tom or Bove? He did come through with B-Rich to upgrade the ship, so time would tell where his loyalties lay. Then there's Jack and Lucy who seem happy to have him in charge. Neither of them cared for Lucus and they were relieved to have him gone even though they were shocked when he was killed.

Then there was the matter of funds. The five hundred thousand credits for rescuing Stella would pay for the upgrades leaving the crew with three thousand credits each. They did buy a share of the Ibex with it, but still, the available credits were too low. Bove had several thousand credits in reserve from his compensation when leaving the Galactic Peacekeeper Force (GPF), but that would only go so far. Selling the medical equipment would help, but he needed a buyer.

A beep broke his thoughts alerting him to an incoming message. His Opticom showed a message from Tom. *What now?* He answered, "Bove here."

"It's Tom," there was a slight pause then he added, "Can we talk?"

"Sure, what's on your mind?"

"Can we meet? I'm at the Brunswick Royal. The bar here's pretty quiet."

"What's this about?"

"I'd rather talk in person. Later today?"

"Is four good?" Bove asked, he could feel the nervous tension in Tom's voice. *This can't be good.*

"Four will work," Tom paused, then added. "Okay."

*        *        *

Bove took an AutoCab to the Brunswick Royal and the twenty-minute ride gave him time to wonder what Tom wanted. He had been quick to agree that Bove should be captain, but was he just going along with the rest of the crew? Was he having second thoughts and wanting the captain's chair? Bove liked being captain, but if the crew backed Tom could he maintain discipline—keep control? He took a deep breath to calm himself, I'll *have to wait and see what he wants*.

The AutoCab came to a stop in front of the hotel and the door slid open. Bove entered the hotel lobby to find a quiet relaxed atmosphere, the few people there sat on comfortable couches or chairs and spoke in soft voices so that Bove could hardly hear them. He scanned the room and on the far side he spotted a doorway with a sign above saying 'Fireside.' *Must be the bar*, he headed toward it. The lights were low in the Fireside, and it took a moment for his eyes to adjust, and when they did, he saw a large fireplace on one wall facing the bar where two couples sat quietly talking. Tables filled the space between the bar and the fireplace and booths lined the other two walls. In the booth farthest from the door he saw Tom nursing a drink. He waved when he saw Bove.

Bove slid in opposite him, "What's up?" He asked.

"You want a drink?" Tom asked.

"I'm good. What's on your mind?"

'I've been thinking," Tom started then stopped worry flickered across his face. "I don't want to cause any trouble, but you just spend all our credits to upgrade the ship and I've been thinking we should get our investment back. I think everyone would agree." Tom leaned forward, "So, how do you plan to reimburse us?" He tapped his fingers on the table.

"What do you think I owe you?"

"Ninety-seven thousand credits. That's what I contributed to the upgrade."

"You want no stock in the ship? I don't know how that would work."

"I want to be independent, to make my own decisions, go where I want. I want off the ship."

"Off?" That was a surprise, and he wondered where this was going. He didn't have the credits to repay him, and Tom knew that. Was he going to suggest that Bove step down and let him have the ship as compensation?

"Yeah, off. It's been too long for me. The only big score we got, and you blow it on an upgrade."

"What's been too long?" Bove had been in command less than two months, which couldn't be too long. Was Tom unhappy with just being on board?

"It's been four years, and the Ibex should be mine now that Lucus is gone. That's what he would have wanted."

"That's not what his *will* said."

"I don't care what his *will* said. He told me I was the best member of the crew. That meant something. Besides the will was old, he probably wrote it before I was on board."

"That doesn't matter, it will stand up against any magistrate as valid," Bove said.

"Whatever," Tom took a drink and set the glass down hard. 'I want my credits. It's not right you used them to upgrade the ship."

Bove cut him off, "Everyone, including you, agreed on the upgrade whatever the cost. You saw the situation we were in with the Black Star. They could have easily taken us out and you know it. These upgrades are for our protection."

"I want no part of it. So, how are you planning to pay me back?"

"I wasn't planning to pay anyone back. We agreed that we would each have a share of the ship, but if you want off, you'll have to wait. I don't have any credits right now. Once we sell the cargo, we will see what we have. That's all I can tell you."

Tom sat back, arms crossed over his chest, staring at Bove, "That's not good enough. You owe me." He leaned forward his hands gripping the edge of the table and lowering his voice, "I want my credits."

"You'll have to wait." Bove stared back at him. "There's no other way."

"I'm not leaving the ship until I'm paid," Tom took another drink and set the glass down, "Can you guarantee you'll pay me?"

"You'll get paid when I have the credits," Bove slid to the edge of the bench ready to get up and leave. "Okay?" He asked.

Tom nodded and watched Bove stand up and walk away. He stayed quiet, eyes on Bove, as he left the bar. Tom took another drink, tipping his head back and closing his eyes.

Dan slid into the booth opposite Tom with a beer in hand. "So, what did he say?" he asked.

"He's not planning to pay any of us back. We're out ninety-seven grand. He claims we all share in the ship, but what's that worth? And the cargo's not going to bring enough to pay all of us."

"We did agree to upgrade the ship, and he said we would share in all profits."

"Profits? How much do you think he can get for the cargo? Maybe two hundred grand. And he doesn't have any idea how to get more." Tom leaned back, eyeing Dan. "We either get out and cut our losses or we take the ship back. He has no stock in it. He's only been with us for a couple of months, not like you and me, or the rest of the crew."

"Jack and Lucy won't go for it. They think he's great." Concern flicked across Dan's face.

"We don't need Jack or Lucy," Tom said and took another drink, then looked Dan in the eye. "If we take him out while the ship is being upgraded it can be explained as an accident, or whatever."

"Take him out? What do you mean? You want to kill him?' Dan pressed back against the seat, shock clear in his eyes. "No, we can't."

"Yeah, we can!" Tom glared at him, "We don't have to kill him, just incapacitate him. You know break a leg or arm, or his head. You get my drift?"

Dan slowly shook his head but said nothing. What Tom was suggesting was not right, it wasn't the way to take the ship. It was illegal and would land them in prison. *No*, he shook his head, *I won't be part of that. And why bother? Bove has been good--upfront with everything. We could have said no to the upgrades, but we didn't. Everyone knew they were needed. No, Tom is being rash not thinking clearly.* Dan pushed the idea away and shook his head again, "That's not right," he said.

"Well, think about it. We have a couple of weeks, and I can put together a plan that's sure to work. Just think about it. Okay?"

Dan nodded, not liking being pushed, and he was sure he couldn't go along with Tom.

*       *       *

Back in his office, Bove put thoughts of Tom away and eased into a soft overstuffed chair. Tom would get his credits when he had them. Pressing more on his mind were the visions he had been experiencing, particularly the latest one. He thought they were over but now after having another, he felt he would never be free of them. He was beginning to understand the situation after the latest one. His commitment wasn't to do the right thing, it was to do the right thing for the Krytheans. Somehow, he must stop or control them, and to do that he had to understand how they worked,

Before the vision on the three hills, he had been in a fight. He had gotten out of control because no one believed they had occurred. The result of the fight was a broken forearm and ankle, bruised ribs, and a swollen eye. Then he had the vision on the three hills.

When he had come out of that vision his broken bones had healed, his bruises gone, and all the swelling cleared up. At the time he was confused and upset about it, but he didn't realize the significance of the healing. Once he had time to think it through, he realized there was not a simple answer. He was unable to explain how it happened.

At first, he thought it was a hallucination perhaps induced by a drug, but there had been no way to introduce a drug into his system. He was alone with Steps on Kryth for ten days when the first visions occurred, so Steps would have had to drug him. Why would he do that? And later he was in the infirmary for his injuries and the doctor or nurse would have had to drug him. Why would they do that? And the latest vision was on the Ibex while he was alone. No, there was no drug involved, so what was driving the visions? And who was behind them?

Dreams were another thought. Dreams can be very real to the point of making you think you are experiencing them, but that wouldn't explain the healing of his broken bones. Bones don't heal in a single day. So, the vision of the three hills had to have taken at least six weeks for the bones to completely heal. How could that be possible? He woke up still in the infirmary with the doctor checking him the day after he was admitted, and everything was healed. It made no sense.

He rubbed his head and pressed his fists against his eyes to help clear his thoughts. He had to know how the visions could be possible. If he understood them, maybe he could control them or prevent them. That would be a relief. "Ooooh," he sighed, *if only. Then maybe they're gone. Maybe I won't have another. One can always hope.*

He closed his eyes hoping for sleep.

# Five

Walter Mitchell, president of the GPF liked to keep his company away from prying eyes, so the headquarters was far from any major city in a five-thousand-acre forest of scarlet oak, sycamore, and shellbark hickory that extended to the horizon. Not many were welcome, but the UEF was an exception being a partner in the colonization project.

Arnold Pencaster and Beau Butler entered the headquarters of the GPF and were escorted to Mitchell's office on the twelfth floor. An overstuffed couch and two matching chairs were arranged on one wall with a serving table next to the couch. Bottles of Sancusian rum, Taz whiskey, Sharian brandy, as well as other spirits lined the lower shelf. On top was a coffee pot, cups, saucers, tea, sugar, et cetera. Opposite the couch was a dark cherry-wood desk in front of a wall of windows giving a breathtaking view.

"Please sit," Mitchell stood pointing to the chairs opposite his desk. "Would you like coffee or tea? A drink?" He asked motioning to Eric Turner, his assistant sitting near the door.

"Thanks, but no," Pencaster said.

"Coffee would be nice," Butler said as he studied Mitchell. "Two sugars."

"Certainly." Mitchell nodded to Turner to take care of it, then turned to Pencaster, "So, what can I do for you," he lowered into his chair while glancing at Butler.

"We have a situation you can help us with. Our new colony on Kryth has been there for the last six months, and now the Kazon Empire claims it is within their territory."

"I see. One of our First Encounter teams studied the ruins there. It was within the scope of our expansion parameters and well outside Kazon territory. They think everything is theirs, particularly any planet close to their empire. So, how can I help?"

Turner sat coffee and pastries on the table next to Butler.

"The Kazons want the colonies moved and implied they would do it themselves if we didn't," Pencaster glanced at Butler concerned that this was not going to be easy.

"Humm. but how does that concern the GPF?" Mitchell felt a shiver run up his back, indicating there was more to this than a simple request for assistance. He didn't need the government interfering with his company even though they did work together to set up colonies throughout the galaxy, but still, it was his company and he wanted to keep a tight rein on the government's influence.

"Your First Encounter teams are perfectly suited for a mission the president has in mind, we're here to discuss options."

Mitchell turned toward Butler, "Please," he gestured to the tray of refreshments. Then directing his attention back to Pencaster, "We don't do government missions."

"Wait," Pencaster raised a hand to stop Mitchell from continuing, "hear us out before you make any rash decisions. Okay?"

Mitchell looked at him, then glanced at Butler. He nodded, "Okay, but still, we don't do government missions, so don't get your hopes up." He leaned back in his chair and crossed his arms over his chest waiting.

"Well," Butler started, "you seem to drive a hard bargain, but, nevertheless, this issue concerns us all. All of us as humans. The Kazons have claimed Kryth as theirs and they say will do whatever it takes to keep it." Butler studied Mitchell for a moment gauging his reaction, then he continued, "We, as a species, can't let any alien decide what's theirs to take. The next thing they would be knocking at our door claiming the Earth belongs to them. Now we can't let that happen, can we?" Butler gazed at Mitchell holding him fixed in his seat. Mitchell didn't react, he took a sip of water, "Go on," he said.

"The President," Pencaster interrupted, "wants to know more about the Kazons. Like what they are capable of and what they are planning. We don't want any surprises."

"And you want to use one of our First Encounter teams?" Mitchell asked.

"They are trained for this kind of operation, and the president thinks they could handle this mission with little problem."

"Just what are you asking our team to do?"

"Not a team," Butler said. "A single agent who could engage the Kazons and find out everything about them and their goals. A simple fact-finding mission, like they routinely do on any planet."

"On a routine mission, there aren't hostiles aware of who we are and ready to take action against us. It seems like a situation that can quickly go wrong." Mitchell sifted his eyes between Pencaster and Butler, questions flashing over his face.

"It's not that kind of assignment," Butler assured him. "There would be no risk."

"There's always a risk." Mitchell leaned forward. "Is this a request? Or an order?"

"The situation is very serious," Butler said, "and it can escalate quickly. We need to know what we're up against, and you are our best hope to find they're capabilities."

Mitchell took a deep breath and pushed back from his desk. 'You want us to give you an agent to infiltrate an alien culture?"

"Isn't that what your agents do?"

"What kind of backlash will that cause us? What rumors will start if this gets out? And it will get out. The government can't keep anything secret." Mitchell stood and turned his back on them looking out the window. "We have colonies all over the galaxy and if they think we're setting up colonies on planets that are not ours. Who knows what that could cause? Rebellion? Like the first set of colonies. We don't need that."

"I understand that," Pencaster said, "and we will do everything to keep this under wraps. We don't want this to get out any more than you do. But your First Encounter teams are highly trained in this very endeavor. They are our best option."

"I don't see how we can help you." Mitchell shook his head knowing Pencaster would find a way to force the issue. The government was good at getting what it wanted, even if it had to force its will. The GPF would have to relinquish its position.

"Actually," Turner broke in, "I think there is a way. You said you wanted a single agent, right?"

Pencaster and Butler looked at Turner, Mitchell turned around to face him wondering what he had in mind.

"Well," Turner continued, there is one agent who might be able to help. He no longer works for the GPF, but he is fully trained."

Mitchell considered Turner, questions flicking across his face, "Who?" he asked.

"Agent Sandle." Turner smiled sitting straighter in his chair.

Mitchell sat and tapped his fingers on the desk. "That's a good idea. Do you have any idea where he is, and do you think he would agree to a mission like that?"

"The right offer might sway him," Turner said.

"What kind of offer are you thinking about?" Pencaster could see a light brightening at the end of the tunnel of resistance and saw hope for an agreement.

Mitchell calculated in his head what Sandle might agree to, then said, "Twenty-five thousand credits might do it."

"Twenty-five, huh? I'll see what I can do. Where can I find this agent Sandle?"

Mitchell looked at Turner, "Eric, do you know where he is?"

"The latest information I have is that he was here on Earth."

"Where exactly?"

"I believe he landed in New Brunswick."

"Can you pin him down? Get contact info?"

"Sure, that won't be a problem."

"Out of curiosity, why do you know his whereabouts?"

"I keep tabs on any former encounter agents in case their skills are needed, like now."

"I see," Mitchell leaned back gazing at Eric, "very good," he smiled.

Pencaster stood up "Okay, he said, "get that info to me ASAP," he took a deep breath, "We'll be in touch." He offered his hand to seal the agreement.

Mitchell shook, and smiled, "Eric will get that to you right away."

"Excellent," Pencaster nodded to Butler.

"Keep us appraised," Butler said as they left the office.

Mitchell looked at Turner, "How soon can you get his contact?"

"By tomorrow," Turner smiled. "I've been keeping track of him thinking he might decide to come back. You know he was one of the best we've had, if not the best."

"Yeah, it's a shame he left. I don't think we could use him though. He's compromised. The visions he claimed to have had disqualified him from active duty. He was assigned to desk duty and would probably stay there if he did come back." Mitchell fell silent in thought for a moment then said, "So, he's in New Brunswick?"

"Yeah. Somehow, he managed to get a ship and some credits and is having the ship upgraded. Where he got the credits, I don't know."

"How about the ship, where did he get that?"

"Don't know that either," Turner said. "But I've heard that the crew all like him and want him to stay with the ship. I guess he's the pilot."

"The ship's not his?"

"I'm not sure. What I've heard is he acts like it's his, but he seems to answer to the crew. So, I don't know what the situation is."

"Is he going to be around very long?"

"He's been here several weeks so he could be leaving anytime."

"Good, get the info together for Pencaster. Let him know how to contact him."

"Will do. He had to register the ship and I'm sure the authorities will have his contact information. It shouldn't be a problem to get,"

"Good, get to it."

"Right away, sir." Turner left to gather the intel for Pencaster.

# Six

From a sound sleep, Bove's Opticom woke him with a soft beep. B-Rich displayed on the caller display, *Problems*, he wondered as he fumbled to answer it. "Yeah," he said, silencing the beep.

"Yo, B-Rich here, how's it going my man?"

"B-Rich, what's up?"

"Got a message for you on your ship's com. Some guy wants to talk to you. He seemed kind of anxious to hear from you, like excited, you know?"

"Who?"

"Don't know. He wasn't very forthcoming. He said to tell you to contact him right away, like right now. Are you in some sort of trouble? Something I can help you with? You know I have contacts that can handle things like this."

"Rich," Bove cut him off, "Did he leave a number or a name?"

"Yeah, he said his name was something like Jim Richardsum—J-Rich—or something like that. He was real formal, ya know, like 'Is Bove Sandle there?' That's why I thought you were in trouble." There was a slight pause. "You're not, are you?"

"Did he leave a number?"

"Yeah, he left a contact. You want it?"

"Send it to me. You said his name is Jim Richardson?"

"Something like that, yeah."

"Okay, thanks..." Bove disconnected and entered the contact B-Rich had sent.

On the first beep, an answer came, "Mister Sandle," the formal voice surprised Bove, "this is James Richerson Deputy of Foreign Affairs."

"Deputy of what?"

"Foreign affairs for the UEF. Do you have a moment to talk?"

"Uh, yeah. What's this about? Is there a problem with our papers?"

"Oh, no. Nothing like that. I have a proposal for you."

"What kind of proposal?"

"It's a delicate situation, something that should be discussed in person. Are you available tonight, say around seven? I'm at the Brunswick Royal."

The man left little room for maneuvering. it sounded more like an order than a request. *Is everybody at the Royal?* Bove wondered, then answered James, "Yeah, I guess I can. Can you tell me more about this proposal?"

"Seven tonight," James said. "In the Oak Conference room," and disconnected.

*That was abrupt,* Bove eased back on his cot and pulled the cover over himself. He wondered if it had anything to do with Tom's request, then thought not. Tom didn't associate with the government. This had to be something else. *Proposal?* Bove had no idea what he would get into.

*      *      *

He found the Oak Conference room on the second floor in the hotel's conference center. *A conference room to meet with me...* Bove felt unsure about this idea, maybe he should just leave, or not, he decided as he pulled open the door.

A large table sat in the center of the room with five men seated around it. At the side of the room, a serving cart sat with coffee and refreshments. Bove glanced around bewildered by the group of men waiting for him.

"Bove, I'm glad you could make it." The man in the center chair stood," I'm James Richerson, and these gentlemen are," he continued gesturing to the other men seated at the table, "Arnold Pencaster, our military Advisor to the president, Beauregard Butler, the general of the Space Force, Walter Mitchell, President of the Galactic Peacekeeper Force, and his assistant, Eric Turner." Before Bove could respond, James continued, "Please help yourself to some refreshments," he pointed to the cart, "and have a seat." He gestured to the chair opposite him.

"It's nice to meet you, Bove." Walter stood up and reached across the table offering his hand to shake.

Bove ignored it, instead, he asked, "Are you waiting for me?" he tried to grasp the meaning of it all. "Is anyone else coming?"

"No, no just you." James said, "Please relax; have a donut--some coffee. No need to worry." James eased back into his chair, reaching his hand towards the chair opposite him.

Bove hesitated then took the seat James had pointed to, "What is this all about?" He asked.

"Well, as I said when we talked, we have a proposal for you," James said. "A mission that includes a sizeable compensation package if you accept." James studied Bove for a moment looking for a response. He saw none so he continued, "We have a situation with Kryth and the Kazon Empire.

"Kryth? And who?" Bove was feeling more concerned about what was coming next. He took a deep breath, crossed his arms over his chest, and leaned back in his chair.

"Okay," James took a breath, "let me fill you in. Kryth, you remember it, the Delta planet of Pheonix-Gamma?" Bove nodded, but before he could say anything, James continued. "The Kazon Empire is near there and they claim the planet has belonged to them for the last twenty-five years, so they are sworn to protect it."

"And how does this concern me?" Bove asked.

James glanced at General Butler, then to Bove, and said, "I'll let General Butler explain."

Beau Butler straightened up in his chair and leaned toward Bove, "This is a mission of galactic importance, son," he said. "A mission that will reshape the nature of the galaxy for years to come, and you, my boy, are the kingpin for its success. You were on the last mission to Kryth, which puts you in a unique position to follow up."

"Are you referring to the visions I had? The visions that showed me the destruction you caused to Kryth? The visions that I should have listened to and not recommended colonization. Is that what you are referring to?" Bove could feel trouble heading his way. The government does not ask things lightly and there are always strings attached no matter how invisible they are. Bove felt a chill run up his back at the government coming to him for help. *This can't be good. I should just leave before they suck me in.* But before he could make a move General Butler caught his attention.

"Destruction? What destruction?" General Butler looked surprised and sat back.

"Didn't you kill off the inhabitants? Destroy the forest?" Bove didn't understand their surprise. The visions had been clear about the destruction, which was why he had committed to redeeming himself. The journey over the three hills was for that purpose and his commitment was to assure him of his redemption. No, Butler was lying, they had destroyed the planet.

"There were no inhabitants," Walter cut in. "Nothing but those ruins you surveyed, which turned out to be from the first colonization over a hundred years ago." He took a deep breath, "And, we don't kill inhabitants. You know that."

Bove's mind whorled. *Was this true? Had there been no destruction as the visions had shown? Were they wrong? Lies? Had he been duped*? "You're saying there were no inhabitants, no destruction? That the ruins were a hundred years old from an earlier colony?"

"That's right," Butler said.

"Back on point," Pencaster interrupted. "What the general is saying. is that we need more information about the Kazon Empire, and that's where you can be effective."

Bove stared at Butler trying to process this new information. No destruction spun around in his head. He had committed because of something that never happened. He didn't have to honor the commitment. He was off the hook.

"Bove?" Pencaster prodded him, "Are you with us?"

"Uh," Bove muttered glancing up at Pencaster," What did you say?"

"We need more information," Pencaster studied Bove and glanced at General Butler.

"Yes," General Butler added, "We need someone, preferably you, to find out as much as possible about their military capabilities."

"Who's capabilities?" Bove asked.

"The Kazons," Butler studied Bove. "Are you with us, son?"

Bove tried to clear his thoughts telling himself the visions would have to wait. He needed to focus. He studied General Butler for a full minute watching his body language as he waited for an answer. "Uh, yeah," he cleared his throat, "I have two questions," he finally said. "First, why me? And second, what's the compensation?"

"Good questions," James said shifting in his chair to get more comfortable. "First the compensation is twenty-five thousand credits to be deposited into your account when the mission is completed. And we want you because you are uniquely qualified to carry out such a mission."

Twenty-five thousand?" Bove tapped his fingers on the table in thought, *The GPF doesn't want to be involved in this, so they are trying to dump it on me for next to nothing. I wonder how much they need me.* He slid back in his chair, glanced at Walter, then looked at Richerson and asked, "Don't you have trained soldiers that can do this?" Then shifting his eyes to Walter asked, "Or doesn't the GPF have other agents as well trained as I am?"

"We have soldiers, yes," General Butler said, "but they aren't trained to meet aliens as you are. Your training is unique in that respect, and we need someone with that expertise to gain information. And you are uniquely qualified to do just that."

"Am I?" Bove let that fall and turned to Walter, "Any of the First Encounter agents are as capable as I am. And," he added, "none are compromised as I am. It seems because of my visions I'm not in the best shape for a mission. So, why me?"

"Well," Mitchell spoke up, "there are other agents with your training, but unfortunately, they're currently unavailable. Out on other missions. And you, Bove, are one of the best agents we have. Uniquely qualified for a mission such as this."

"So," James said, "that leaves you, and twenty-five thousand credits. A lot of compensation, don't you agree?"

"You know I don't work for the GPF any longer," Bove said while thinking twenty-five thousand wasn't much for the crew. Five thousand each. No, he needed a hundred thousand for each crew member— half a million. *This is a bust*, he studied Richerson. *They will never go for half a million.*

"That's not an issue," Walter interrupted smiling at Bove, "as far as we are concerned you never left. We've kept your file open just waiting for your return."

"What?" Bove couldn't believe what he had just heard. His file was still open waiting for him to return. He didn't know if he wanted to, not after the way they had treated him. They had made it clear that he was on desk duty for the duration of his employment. "Return to full duty?" He asked.

"Of course," Walter smiled at Bove, "We believed you would be back in the field in no time. It will be just a few administrative steps for you to be back on full duty. How does that sound?"

"So, that aside," Butler took over, "what we need is someone with your skills to gather information about the Kazons." He looked at Bove assessing his mood, then continued, "Listen, son, this has galactic implications now and in the future. You will be doing this for your world, for the planet you explored and deemed suitable for colonization. This is for you and the world. For our future. We must protect our own!"

*This is a hard sell.* He couldn't believe the GPF wanted him back, or that he was the only choice. Something else was going on and he wasn't sure if he wanted any part of it. "Why," he asked, "can't you wait for an active team to be freed up? I've been inactive for over six months. Not the most up-to-date agent for the job. It seems a better choice would be an active team that's in shape and ready for this kind of assignment. Am I wrong?"

"Well, yes you are," James glanced around the table. "You see this is time-sensitive and top secret. If it gets out that we are investigating another civilization, there could be protests. And no matter how unwarranted they are we will still get a black eye. So, we need to keep this under wraps for the time being. That's why you are the best choice, you see?"

"I don't think this is possible," Bove said, "this would put my crew in danger, and I won't allow that. And," he went on, "twenty-five K is not a reasonable amount. There're five members in my crew and each would be in the same danger as me. They'll need compensation also."

"So," James said, "you're saying you will do this for a hundred and twenty-five K?"

"No," Bove stood to leave, "I'm saying you can count me out."

"Wait," James said standing up, "a hundred and twenty-five thousand credits is a lot, don't you think?"

"Yes, it's a lot." Bove agreed. "But not enough. If you want me to go into a hostile environment to gain information, I'll need a lot more than that."

"How much more?"

"I have a crew of five, six, counting me. Putting my crew in danger will cost you a hundred each, plus expenses."

"Expenses? What are you talking about?"

"It's not cheap flying across the galaxy. And flying into hostile territory will require that I arm the crew and supply protective gear. That too is not cheap. So, that's what I mean when I say expenses."

James sat back in his chair and looked at Bove with a slight smile on his face. "You are quite the negotiator, but I'm not at liberty to authorize that amount. A hundred twenty-five K is our limit. If you feel that's not acceptable, then we can't do business."

"Okay," Bove said. "It was nice talking to you." He turned and stepped towards the door.

James was surprised at Bove's response. He was assured that twenty-five would be enough and only had the authority to go to a hundred. But Bove was the only choice, he was unconnected from the Force and not working for the government which makes him perfect to go into enemy territory to gather information. If caught they would have no liability. He would be considered a rogue citizen acting on his own. He had to accept. "Are you sure about this?" He asked.

"Yes," Bove reached for the door.

"I'm not authorized, but maybe my superior can help. Won't you sit while I contact him?"

Bove turned facing James, "If you have to ask for agreement, ask for seven hundred."

James looked up laying his communicator on the table. "Seven?" he asked, blinking his eyes, and clearing his throat. "Are you serious?"

"Yes. Seven or I walk." Bove sat.

James finished his call in five minutes and told Bove they agreed that six hundred thousand credits would be deposited into his account on completion of the mission. Bove told him that was not acceptable, and that half would be due when he accepted, provided his crew agreed. And the rest after the mission. James agreed with the stipulation that they leave right away.

"My ship is being upgraded," Bove said. "We'll leave when it's ready." He stood and as he turned toward the door to leave, he smiled to himself, ninety-seven thousand to Tom, and a hundred for each of the crew. Now he needed to get their agreement.

"You have two days to let me know," James said. "And you didn't say when your ship would be ready to leave."

It was a question Bove needed to answer. "Two days is fine," he said. "A week for the ship."

"Make it faster," James said.

*Great*, Bove grabbed the door handle, *already they're making demands*. "I'll see what I can do, but we'll leave when it's ready." He said and left.

# Seven

He returned to his office hoping to get a good night's sleep; he was tired from the stress of the day and the offer kept circling in his mind. It supplied an answer to Tom's request, but it could be dangerous.

It was Tom he wondered about, was he planning to leave the ship, striking out on his own, or did he have other plans? If he left, they would need a replacement, meaning more time earthside--time that he didn't have now. He had agreed to leave the minute the upgrades to the Ibex were completed. If Tom left, they would make do and replace him at the end of the mission.

As he began to drift into a quiet sleep when suddenly a voice jerked him awake. "You did well with Stella," the voice said. Bove sat up and found himself in a familiar room, covering the opposite wall were curtains of red and green flowers on a light blue background. The other walls had murals of trees; animals wandered the ground among them and in the treetops birds perched. The ceiling was a blue sky scattered with soaring birds and puffy clouds. Sitting across from him were two familiar figures—Tanka and Kabluff.

"Where am I..." Bove voiced yet he knew he was in the final temple of his journey over the three hills. It was during that journey that Bove committed to doing the right thing regardless of the risk to himself. It was because of that commitment that he rescued Stella from Zabi.

"You have reached a critical time," Kabluff said, "and you have an opportunity to change the course of events leading to the future. You committed to doing what is required to prevent chaos and now the opportunity is here to shape the future." Kabluff studied Bove for a few moments, his eyes boring into his mind as if he were reading his thoughts.

"Would you like some water?" Tanka asked.

"What?" Bove tried to focus. "This is another vision," he said. "A vision I don't want, and advice I don't need."

"You must learn the consequences of your actions," Kabluff said smiling at Bove. "Have a drink," he took a cup of water from Tanka and headed it to Bove.

Bove took a sip remembering how sweet the water was while crossing the three hills. Remembering the perils he faced and the commitments he made. He took another sip.

"Relax, listen, and learn. The proposal you are offered gives you a reason to do as we request. You will be on Ardonia, the Kazon home world, and will have the opportunity to speak with them—to persuade them to leave Kryth alone. You must ease tensions that will develop between Earth and the Kazons. You must calm the Kazons, make them see the folly of their actions."

"What?" Bove asked shaking his head. He looked at Kabluff, then Tanka. "Why should I believe you? I asked about Kryth and the destruction of their civilization and found it wasn't true. You had lied to me. There was no one on the planet. The ruins were from a failed Earth colony. All the destruction you showed me was a lie." Bove took a breath, and before anyone could respond, he continued, "And these visions. What are they? What I experienced was not real. This is not real. I don't even know if you're real. You could be a phantom created in my mind."

"I assure you," Kabluff said, "we are very real." He gave Bove a chance to process this, and then he continued, "Our intent was not to mislead you, but to show you the destruction of Kryth to convince you to reject the colonization. To prevent the current situation from occurring. Unfortunately, it didn't work and now we find ourselves facing a crisis."

"Why should I believe you now? And what am I supposed to do? All I'm asked to do is gather information. How will that change anything."

"You must do more than that, you must prevent an escalation that can lead to war." Kabluff stared into Bove's eyes, "You see if Kryth had not been colonized the Kazons would not be claiming it as theirs, and we would have no issues. But because you recommended colonization, we now have a crisis. A crisis caused by your failure!"

"I failed at nothing!" Bove glared at Kabluff, fingers curled into fists, and a desire to strike him flooded his mind. They had lied and made him commit to do their bidding based on that lie. "And my commitments are void. My redemption is void. I owe you nothing."

"Bove," Kabluff interrupted, "you must consider what's at stake."

"I must do nothing of the sort."

"There's always the bog as an option," Tanka said.

Bove took a breath. Stood and walked away from them. "How would you explain my disappearance?"

"That's not our concern," Kabluff said and smiled at Bove. "Our concern is stopping this situation from escalating and making sure you do your part. The Kazons will want your colonists off their planet, and you must keep them from forcing the issue."

"But it's not their planet." Bove protested."

"It doesn't matter," Kabluff said. "You must accept the proposal, meet with the Kazons, and make peace."

"And if I refuse?"

"You won't, and you know it. You need the credits, and you don't want the bog."

"I'm leaving this vision now," Bove stated and tried to force the vision to disappear. Tried to return to his office. He closed his eyes thinking of his cot, forcing his thoughts to return to the real world where things made sense. To the world where he was comfortable in bed, on Earth. Flashes of the ship appeared in his thoughts. He could sense the environment he wished to be in, the smell of the city, the heaviness of the air, the sounds around him—AutoCabs passing, people talking, the humming of environmental controls. Then it was gone. He opened his eyes to see Tanka and Kabluff watching him.

"Do you understand what must be done?" Kabluff glanced at Tanka, serious lines etching his forehead.

"I understand what you're saying." Bove said running his fingers through his hair, "But I don't trust you. I'll do what they ask to earn the credits, but you'll have to find someone else to be your peacemaker."

"The bog is the cost of your refusal. Success brings peace. You must decide which it will be."

Kabluff waved his hand in an arc, and Bove woke, a bit dazed and uncertain of what had happened. *Did I dream of a vision with Kabluff?* He wondered, knowing it was not true.

*    *    *

Morning dawned with sunlight streaming through the window into Bove's eyes. Covering his face, he rolled to his side out of the light. Sleep had been elusive as the vision replayed in his thoughts mingling with those of the proposal.

He sat up and pushed the vision from his mind. The proposal had to be discussed. On the surface, it seemed a simple task, yet there were risks. For one he didn't know anything about the Kazons and before agreeing he needed more information. Then there was the push from Richerson for an answer in two days. Bove felt that once he agreed there would be no alternative but to complete it.

Accepting the proposal would solve Tom's request for his credits, and since he felt uneasy with Tom, paying him off would be a relief. But before that could happen the crew must agree to accept the proposal. He sent a message requesting everyone to join a conference call at six. Next, he needed to know when the ship would be ready, so he selected B-Rich on his Opticom and called him.

"Yo," B-Rich yelled into the receiver. "What's happening man?"

"B-Rich, it's Bove."

"Yeah, I know. What's up?"

"What's the status of the ship."

"It's looking good, man. I was going to call you to let you know we're almost finished, just a day or two, maybe three. But it's coming along just fine. I was able to get everything you asked for and it's working great. It's like a new ship. You're going to be very happy. Yeah, we're moving right along."

"Good. When will it be completed? You've had it for over six weeks now."

"Yeah, yeah, I know. I told you it would be six to eight weeks, right? So, I'm ahead of schedule."

"How do you figure?"

"We're looking at the end of next week," B-Rich said.

"I need it sooner. Can you finish by tomorrow?"

"Not tomorrow," there was a long pause, then B-Rich said. "I'll have to push another job, but yeah I can finish by the end of the week."

"Okay. We're going to have a meeting on the ship in a day or two. Will that interfere with your work?"

"No, no, that's fine. We'll be in the engine compartment. You're not meeting there, are you?"

"No, we'll be on deck two in the conference room."

"Yeah? Okay." B-Rich disconnected.

*The end of the week*, Bove smiled, *that should make James happy.*

# Eight

Bove sat his Opticom in the middle of the desk and connected to the conference call. A holoimage of himself appeared above a small circle before him. Around the desk, small holoimage circles appeared-- one for each crew member. As he waited for them to sign in, he considered how to broach the issue, and decided to take the direct approach by telling them the mission and the pay.

The circle to his right flickered and the image of Jack, the navigator, appeared. "Am I the first?" he asked, knowing the answer. "Is the ship done?"

"We'll wait for everyone," Bove said looking at Jack's image.

After a short wait, all the circles were reflecting the images of the crew members. Lucy appeared next to Jack. Across from Jack, Dan appeared with Tom next to him. Ryan was the last, appearing across from Bove. As each appeared they had asked the same question, and Bove gave the same answer. But now that everyone had signed in, he could explain the purpose of the call. He started with a simple statement.

"I have been offered a project by the Deputy of Foreign Affairs for the UEF."

Before he could continue, Tom interrupted him, "The Deputy of Foreign Affairs? What does he want with us?" skepticism showed in his voice.

Bove leaned back in his chair, glanced around the table at the images, and decided Tom was the only one concerned. Everyone else seemed to want to hear what the project was about. "The government wants us to gather information about the Kazon Empire," he said.

"What?" Dan almost yelled but held his voice in check. "That's not a good idea. Do you know what the Kazons are like?" And before anyone could answer he continued, "I do. I've dealt with them in the past and they're cruel. Unforgiving and think they rule the galaxy. I would stay as far away from them as possible."

Bove was taken back. He took a deep breath, leaned forward, and placed his elbows on the desk. He checked each crew member for a reaction. Everyone else was silent. yet concerned. "Okay," he said, "we'll get back to that." He glanced at everyone again. "They want us to find out about their intentions concerning Kryth, the Delta planet of Phoenix-Gamma."

"Kryth? Wasn't that your last assignment?" Tom asked.

"Yeah, but that has nothing to do with this," Bove glared at him thinking he was going to make an issue of it.

"Right," Tom's voice oozed sarcasm. "And why does the government want to know what the Kazons are doing concerning Kryth?"

"Kazon claims it's in their territory, and they want the colonists removed. We are to get information about their plans and capabilities." Bove explained.

"How are we going to do that?" Tom asked.

"We'll set up a trade agreement," Bove said.

"And trade what?" Dan interrupted.

"Something they desperately need. But we're getting ahead of ourselves, we need to decide if we want to accept this or not. It pays six hundred thousand credits by the way."

The room fell silent. Jack let out a breath, "Wow!" he said.

"That's a hundred each," Lucy said.

"Well, that puts another consideration on the table, doesn't it?" Dan observed.

"Yeah," Tom agreed, glancing at Dan.

Ryan just glanced around at the others, and said, "A hundred."

"I have to let them know by tomorrow night if we accept or not." Bove said, "So, what do we need to know to make a decision?"

"Well, according to Dan, we may want to stay as far from them as we can." Jack said, "But still, a hundred grand is a lot of credits."

"I think," Bove said, "we need more information about the Kazons. So, Dan get everything you know about them."

"Okay," Dan said frowning and running a hand over his head. "Ardonia, the Kazon home world, is near the Ceti system, and that's one of our colonies. So why aren't they claiming that too?"

"Don't know," Bove said, "maybe because Kryth's closer. Lucy, see what you can find out about them. We'll get together tomorrow and make a decision. One more thing, the ship will be ready by the end of the week, so we'll meet on board in the conference room. Deck two, Ryan. I plan to leave next week."

Everyone acknowledged and disconnected.

*Ceti-2, Stella's world, is close to the Kazons, so would she know something about them?* Bove felt a flush at the thought of her. After the rescue which saved her life, Bove felt she owed him a favor despite the generous compensation. So, he would contact her for help, and being close to the Kazons she should have information that could help him. Plus, he wanted to see her again, not that there was anything between them, but he wanted to see. After her abrupt departure last time, he wondered if she would even want to meet with them. *We'll see...*

*              *              *

Dan slid into the seat across from Tom in the hotel bar.

"Well?" Tom asked.

Dan set his whiskey and seven on the table between them. "Well, what?" he asked glaring at Tom and raising his hands, palms up.

Tom slid back in his seat and straightened up, he took a sip of his rum and Coke, "What'd you think of Bove's proposal? Are you going to agree to take it?"

"It's a lot of credits."

"That's not what I asked," Tom leaned forward, "If everyone else agrees I'll go along. It's more credits for me and, it will give us more time to do something about Bove and the ship." He studied Dan's reaction hoping for a favorable nod, or other sign that he agreed with him.

Dan finished his drink and slid out of the booth, "I'll think about it," he said and left.

Tom pushed on the table and clamped his jaw, then drained his glass in one long drink. "Damn," he muttered.

*              *              *

Early the next morning Bove woke from a pleasant dream, stretched, and said, "Well," to no one. The idea of seeing Stella again excited him but he held that feeling in check. *If she doesn't feel the same, then what's the point? But then maybe she does.* He stretched again and made himself a cup of coffee pushing thoughts of Stella away. *We need any information she might have...*

His thoughts returned to the proposal and the reaction of the crew. They seemed pleased with the amount, but Dan's comment concerned him. *Did they take it as a warning and won't want anything to do with the Kazons?* He worried. Then in a more positive frame of mind, he considered that if everyone agreed to accept the proposal, Tom could be paid off and released from the ship. That would be a good thing. Bove had an uneasy feeling about Tom's motives and how they would affect the rest of the crew. This proposal sounded dangerous enough without having internal problems. The sooner Tom left, the better, but would Tom agree to that? If he stayed, he would earn another hundred thousand credits in addition to the ninety-seven thousand he wanted. *How do I handle that,* he wondered.

After finishing his morning coffee, he considered another possibility. He could put Tom's request to the crew and let them decide if he should go or stay. But only after he gets an agreement on the proposal. He nodded to himself. *Next week, we can take a test flight and if everything looks good, we'll be ready to leave.* It felt good to have that settled, one less thing to worry about.

# Nine

The conference room on deck two was once a bare room with only a table and eight swivel chairs in rails. It was meant only for meeting with the crew, but Bove felt it needed decoration, so he obtained pictures – landscapes and still life—to make the room feel welcoming and comfortable, more friendly. He hoped that would help the crew be more open to discussions and ideas.

At nine o'clock he sat at the head of the table waiting for everyone to arrive. *What will they decide?*

Jack came in and slid a chair out, "So, the ship's ready?" He ran his hand through his blond hair pushing it back from his face. "I thought I saw them still working."

Before Bove could answer, Lucy joined them. Her hair was shorter, shoulder length, and curled around her face. The brown highlights accented her brown eyes which glowed when she turned to Jack and said, "Hi."

He smiled, "Hi."

"They're finishing up," Bove answered Jack's question, "we'll be ready to leave next week." He pushed his chair away from the table and leaned back stretching his legs out.

Tom came in. "Everybody here?" He glanced at Jack and Lucy and lowered his six-foot-one-inch frame into the chair. A sour grin spread across his face.

"Not yet," Jack said.

"I see," Tom glanced at Bove.

Dan and Ryan came in and took seats, Dan gave Tom a nervous glare.

Bove noted it, then said. "I need to let the Deputy--James--know our decision on the proposal by six today. So, we need to decide what to do. But let's see what we know first. Dan, what did you find?"

"The one time I dealt with them was six years ago. I was in the service on a star cruiser when we came across a Kazon ship. Same class as us and we were well outside their borders. So, this Kazon ship hales us and says we are illegally inside Kazon territory and if we don't retreat, they will consider it a hostile threat and take whatever action necessary to remove us."

"What'd you do?" Lucy asked.

"Well, the captain didn't take that very well. He says back to them, 'We're well outside Kazon territory, and both our navigation records show that, so if you take any action to move us it'll be considered an act of war, and we'll respond accordingly.'"

"What'd they do?" Jack asked.

"They sent back, 'This is the only warning you will receive. Consider yourself on notice.' And our captain sent back, 'I have dispatched a message stating your threat to both of our higher commanders and I am waiting for a response of what action to take. You should hear something soon.'"

"So?" Jack pushed.

"So, they left the area, and that was the end of it." Dan tapped the tabletop with his knuckles. "So, I'd stay away from them."

"Even for a hundred K?" Jack asked.

"Well, that's a consideration," Dan nodded and glanced at Tom.

"What did you find, Lucy?" Bove wondered what the interaction between Dan and Tom was about. *Trouble?*

"Not a lot. They're confrontational and tend to think everything is theirs. They let very few non-Kazons onto their world. You need something special to get their interest." She stopped and shuffled around in her seat.

"Go on," Bove pushed her.

"Well," she took a deep breath, "They're not like us."

"How do you mean?" Ryan asked.

"Well, they evolved from cats much the way we evolved from apes. So, they resemble cats."

"Like how?" Dan asked, then added, "We never saw them. I thought they were like us."

"Well, they're not," Lucy said. "They have fur covering their faces and ears on the top of their heads. Their feet, well, the lower part of their legs are very big. You know how a cat's back legs have joints that are backward from ours? Well, theirs serve as their ankles making their feet, or the lower part of their leg, big. And they stand on them. But more than that, they have retractable claws on both their hands—paws—and feet and very sharp teeth. Their faces are cat-like with strange eye color—like gold, or dark green."

"Scary, but they are civilized," Jack said more than asked.

"Do you know anything about them?" Tom asked.

Jack shook his head, "No, I just assume they're not animals."

"Sounds like they are," Tom said, "With fur, and claws."

"Enough of that," Bove cut in. "What about their military? Their defenses? Their trading?" He asked Lucy.

"They trade only if someone can offer something they need. They have a security ring around all of their worlds and anyone wanting to land must go through the ring. I didn't find anything about their military. That's top secret. I did find out that weapons are one of the things they'll trade,"

"Okay," Bove said. "That's a great help. At least we know what we will be getting into." He took a deep breath, and glanced around the table, "Any comments, questions?"

"I don't know about this," Ryan said. "I didn't expect to be going into a dangerous environment."

"This is no different than the revolutions you were involved in, is it?" Bove pointed out.

Ryan considered that for a moment, then nodded, "Yeah, I guess you're right."

"So, are you okay?"

"Yeah, I guess," he rubbed his head and looked down.

"What about everyone else?"

"So," Jack said, "what are we supposed to find out?"

"All I know is that they want information," Bove said. "And they want us to start immediately."

"Yeah," Jack said, "But what information?"

"Information about their plans for Kryth. They, the Kazons, sent a demand to remove our colonists. Our government wants to know if they plan to remove them and if they are capable of following through." Bove said.

"So," Tom cut in, "they want to know what the Kazons are planning and their military capabilities."

"That's about right," Bove said, He looked around the table, "We don't know a great deal about them, but from Dan's encounter, they sound like bullies. Big talk and little action. They're suspicious of outsiders, but if we have something they need they should be receptive to trade. Is that about right?" Everyone nodded. "So, assuming we can get weapons for them, or something they need, we should be able to set up a trade agreement. That said, we need to decide if we accept the proposal or not." He glanced around the table again. "Lucy, what do you think?"

"I don't know," she said. "Like Dan said, gathering information is dangerous. If we do this, we'll need a plan."

"Why isn't the GPF doing this?" Jack asked glancing at everyone, then back to Bove.

"Good question," Bove said. "They say there's no one available. All their teams are engaged." He paused for a second and then asked, "Dan, what are your thoughts?"

"About the Kazons? Well, they did back down when we stood up to them, so maybe they are not so bad. And for a hundred K, I think it's worth it. So, I'm in."

"Ryan, you in?"

Ryan nodded, "If we find what they need, I'll go along."

"Once we're committed and, on our way, there's no place to drop you. So, you need to be sure." Bove told him.

Ryan nodded.

"So?" Bove pushed him.

"Yeah, I'm in." he nodded again.

"Kryth," Tom said, "the planet where your last mission was?"

Bove's shoulders tightened in anticipation of trouble. He turned to Tom, "Yes," he said and waited for anything further from him, but Tom just nodded. "Okay," Bove continued, "so it's an information-gathering mission. Shouldn't be too hard."

"You think they'll just offer up what we ask for?" Tom asked.

"No, we'll have to be more discrete, but we can do it." Bove waited for more questions.

"How long will this take?" Dan asked.

"I don't know," Bove shrugged, "it depends on how forthcoming they are. We could get what we need in a couple of days, or it could take a month. Who knows?"

Ryan shifted and he crossed his arms over his chest.

"I think we should accept," Jack said. "We're not at war and they do trade with some people. If we find something they really need we stand a good chance of getting in with them. So, I think we should accept."

Lucy nodded, "If everyone else is going, I'm going too. I won't be left behind."

"So, everyone agrees we do the project?" Tom took over. "We know what we need to find out. I'll put a plan together." He turned to Bove, "You go make sure the ship's ready. Everyone prepare to leave first of the week." Tom looked around the table and then pushed his chair back to leave, "Let's get to it."

No one moved or said a word, they sat waiting.

"Tom," Bove said glancing at the crew. Tom stopped and looked back at Bove. "As captain of this ship, I'll decide when we leave. And I'll make the work assignments. Understood?" Bove held his gaze on Tom, his face blank of expression, yet firm.

Anger flashed across Tom's face, "The crew agreed with me, I should be in charge of the mission. That's all I'm saying, and they agree with me. Right?" He turned to the crew waiting for an answer.

"I agree we do the project," Lucy said, "not because you have anything to say about it, but because Bove has given us the choice to decide, unlike Lucus who never did. Unlike you, Tom." Tom glared at her and started to say something, but she cut him off. "We need a good plan, and everyone will contribute to it." She said emphasizing *everyone*.

Tension hung in the room like morning fog over a lake.

"Tom," Bove said, "verify the cargo we have. I want a list by morning."

Tom glared at him and then turned to Dan ready to say something, but Dan spoke first. "We're all with you, Captain," he said to Bove and glanced at Tom.

"Anything else?" Jack shifted in his chair.

"I'll let James Richerson know our decision," Bove said. "Then we'll make plans. Also, we'll make a test run first of next week when B-Rich is finished. So, everyone hang around, I'll be in touch."

They all nodded in relief and started heading out.

Bove waited until everyone was gone and sighed. *This is going to be hard*," he thought, *but by tomorrow I'll have Tom's credits and he can go his own way.*

*          *          *

At six that evening Bove met with James Richerson and the others. They sat around the same table in the same conference room in the Brunswick Royal Hotel.

"So?" James Richerson asked.

"Half up front, like we agreed?"

"We've drawn up papers just to clarify our agreement. You'll need to sign them before any credits exchange hands." James pushed a sheet of paper across the table to Bove.

"What's this?" Bove picked up the paper and looked it over. It appeared no different from what they had agreed to—Six hundred thousand credits, half on acceptance and half on completion. Bove would provide all information gathered to the Deputy within two days of arriving back on Earth. He saw no issue with signing it, so he did.

Sliding it back to James, he said, "You'll send me a copy?"

James nodded, "Of course."

Bove pulled a folded paper from his pocket and handed it to James. "I want to have ninety-seven thousand credits deposited in this account tomorrow when I contact you," he pulled out another and held it out, "and the rest deposited in this account."

"Not a problem," James said.

When Bove left he cleaned out the office and moved everything to the Ibex. He was done with Earth and ready to be gone. *Next week we will be ready to head out for Ceti-2 and Stella.* He smiled to himself. He had missed her since dropping her off after the rescue. He hadn't thought about her, yet he felt something was missing. He told himself there was nothing there and he thought he was fooling himself that she thought about him. But secretly he hoped he was right.

# Ten

Two days later Bove met with B-Rich about the upgrades. He nodded as B-Rich explained the changes to the ship and showed Bove the new stuff. They agreed on payment once Bove was satisfied that everything was working properly and there were no issues. Bove contacted the crew for a meeting aboard the Ibex in the conference room of deck two.

He sat at the head of the table waiting for everyone to arrive. He thought about Tom's request for his credits and called the meeting to tell him he had his credits so he could leave. But if he refused and tried to take control, the crew could decide his fate. If they let him stay Bove would have to put him in his place for good, he would make it clear any subordination would not be tolerated.

Lucy and Jack entered and took seats next to Bove.

"What is this about?" Jack asked.

"Mission planning," Bove leaned back stretching his legs out.

Lucy glanced at Jack, then said, "Is Tom joining us?"

Bove looked at her, "Why do you ask?"

"Well, it's just that he's been grumbling that the ship should be his." Lucy glanced at Jack again, then continued. "But we all agreed that you should be in charge."

"And the ship belongs to everyone? Right?" Bove asked.

"Yeah," Lucy blushed and shifted in her chair. "But Tom thinks differently."

"How so?"

"Well, he thinks Lucus would have left the ship to him because they were so close."

"Apparently not that close," Bove answered. "The paperwork Lucus left said the ship was to belong to the crew. That means it belongs to all of us—Tom included."

Tom entered just as Bove finished speaking. "What's up?" He stared at Bove for a moment then turned to Jack.

"We're waiting," Lucy said.

"Waiting for what?" Tom said glancing at Bove again. He pulled out a chair and sat glaring at Lucy.

Dan came in, looked around the room, and selected a seat at the end of the table. "Has something happened?" He shifted in his chair glancing at Tom, then toward Bove.

"Nope," Bove said, "When Ryan gets here, we'll start." The room grew silent, everyone shifted in their chairs glancing around, avoiding looking at Tom.

Ryan entered and sat next to Tom. He looked around the table, "Something going on?" he asked.

"Nothing," Bove said. "We're here to make plans for the mission. This is what I propose."

But before he could continue Tom interrupted, "Everyone should have a say in the plans and not just accept your ideas. Don't you all agree?" He turned to the crew expecting them to agree with him.

Lucy spoke up, "Tom, let's hear what he suggests."

"Does he even have a plan?" Tom snapped at her.

"That's what we're about to hear," Jack looked at Tom with disgust. "So why don't you pipe down and listen?"

Tom started to say something, but Bove stopped him, "Tom!" He said, "Drop it. All of you." He stared at each person without wavering. Once everyone had settled down, he continued. "We need to learn more about the Kazons, and we need to find something they want."

"Why don't you do that," Tom interjected, "find out what they want, then we might have a real plan. What do you all think?" He turned to the crew sitting straighter in his chair to give an air of authority.

Lucy stood up pushing her chair back and laying her hands on the table. She leaned over, looked Tom in the face, and said, "We agree that we need more information, but Bove will decide how to get it. You may think you have all the answers, but you're all talk and little substance. At least Bove asked for our input, something Lucus never did. He decided to deliver Stella to Zabi without a word to us. We all could have been killed and you stood by and let it happen. Right!?"

Tom pushed his chair back from the table and glanced around the room.

"Right?" Lucy's eyes narrowed; her lips pressed into a tight line.

Tom looked at Dan, who glanced away, then he turned to Bove. "That's not the point," his voice rose.

"That's exactly the point," Lucy said loudly. "You don't want input. You want control," she stood up straight and glanced away from Tom. "Now let's hear what Bove has to say." She dropped back into her seat.

Tom said no more, he glanced at Bove.

"We are going to Ceti-2," Bove said.

"What? Why?" Dan asked.

"Because it's close to Kazon territory, and they know the Kazons better than any of us," Bove said. "And Stella's there."

"Of course," Tom interjected getting his nerve back. "He wants to see his girlfriend. Are you going to stand for this?" he asked everyone.

Lucy glared at him, "Yes," she said before anyone else could get a word in.

"Stella owes us a favor after we saved her from Zabi," Bove said, "Don't you think, Tom?"

Anger flashed on Tom's face. "Yeah, she owes us!"

"And she may know what they need that we can trade. That will give us an in with them."

The crew nodded around the table, except Tom.

"Once we have set up a trade agreement, we can talk to them. Find out what they're planning to do about Kryth." Bove glanced around the table waiting for agreement.

Tom pushed his chair back, "This sounds rather iffy, no real plan." He started to stand.

Dan shifted in his chair, crossing his arms over his chest but stayed quiet.

"Tom, sit down," Bove demanded.

Tom sat, "The GPF should be handling this not us. We're not a military ship."

"Tom," Bove said, "It doesn't matter about the GPF, and we already know why they're not involved." Bove looked at Tom, then around the room. "So, does everyone agree with this plan?" Everyone nodded.

"Yeah, fine," Tom stood to leave, "Some plan."

"One more thing," Bove said reaching his hand out toward Tom's chair.

Tom looked at Bove anger etched on his face, "What now?" He demanded.

"Sit!" Bove ordered him. From Tom's reaction to Bove's suggestion and the crew's reaction to Tom, Bove decided it was time to see if the crew wanted him to stay.

The crew shifted in their seats. Dan looked at Bove with an open mouth like he wanted to say something but closed it without a word. Tom flopped into his seat.

Everyone was tense, silent, and ready for a confrontation. Bove could feel it like a storm cloud overhead ready to wreak havoc on the world. "Okay," he said breaking the silence. "Tom has requested his investment in the ship's upgrade returned and he wants to leave the ship."

A sigh of relief came from everyone. *They all knew, typical.*

"I may have changed my mind about that," Tom glanced at Dan, "I think you need me for this mission."

Bove ignored Tom's remark, "Let's put this to a vote," he said, "Yea to let Tom go, nay to keep him. Dan let's start with you."

Dan shifted in his seat, rubbed his brow as if sweat were beading there, and glanced at Tom. "Uh," he said.

"I don't think this is up to a vote," Tom spoke up. "I think it's my decision if I want to stay or not."

"Tom," Bove said, "You asked for your credits back so you could go your own way. I'm doing what you asked, and I'm asking for the crew's input. But I wonder why the change." Bove stared at him, then turned to Dan, "And you Dan, what do you know about this?"

"Uh," Dan said again glancing at Tom, "Nothing."

"That's not true," Tom almost shouted, but took a breath and gripped the edge of the table. "You know I want to stay."

"Why?' Bove asked again. "To get more credits?"

Tom blanched, pushed from the table, and stood. "You just want me gone because you know the ship should be mine. Everyone knows it, right?" Tom looked around the table at everyone, but no one spoke. "Dan, tell him," Tom insisted.

"Tell him what? That you want to take the ship? That you are planning to oust him? Is that what you want me to say?" Dan glared at Tom, "I won't help you. You're on your own."

"Is that true, Tom?" Bove stared directly at him.

"Uh," Tom said stepping back from the table toward the door.

"Sit!" Bove stated with no doubt in that single word, "Who's for letting Tom go?"

Four *yeas* sounded, and Bove added softly, "Yea."

Tom backed against the door with a look toward Dan that could kill. "So," he said. "That's the thanks I get after everything I've done for you?" He looked at each crew member. "I've been on this ship longer than any of you and you know Lucus wanted me to have it. You know he thought of me as his equal."

Everyone was silent.

"Fine!" Tom's voice rose almost to a shout. "Fine!" He turned to Bove, "When do I get my credits?"

"They'll be in your account tomorrow," Bove said. "In the meantime, you can get your things off the ship."

"Right," Tom turned and left.

"Anything else?" Jack stood to leave.

"When will we do a test run?" Lucy asked.

"Monday, be ready by eight. Take the rest of the week to get anything you need."

Everyone nodded in relief and Dan got up to leave.

"Make sure Tom gets safely off the ship," Bove said before Dan reached the door. "Jack, help him."

Dan stopped and turned to Bove, relief washing over his face, "I'll make sure he's gone," he said.

# Eleven

The captain's chair of the Ibex had new controls in the arms giving a view of the ship's overall status at a glance. Bove nodded with satisfaction as he studied the information available to him. He checked the crew. To his left was Lucy busy at the computer terminal, and directly in front of him was Jack, with Ryan to his left in the pilot's chair. On the right side of the bridge was Dan taking control of the weapons and cargo, double duty since Tom was gone.

On the arms of the chair, he was able to watch the status of the diagnostics and he smiled as the lights for each system turned green. True to his word, B-Rich had completed the work when he said he would. He had installed the latest transit drive capable of doing a transit in less than a second by entering a destination and pressing the transit command, a vast improvement over the hour it took to activate the old drive. Top-of-the-line weapons covered the front, back, both sides, top and bottom of the ship. Long-range sensors would detect activity as far away as a light year to help decide if there is a threat or not. Overall, the new Ibex was comparable to any military ship currently active.

The diagnostics looked good, but flying the ship and using the transit drive, sensors, and weapons was another test that needed to be completed before Bove was willing to pay B-Rich anything.

"We're going to establish an orbit, then go to the asteroids to test the weapons, and then after we clear the system, we'll transit to Alpha-Centauri to evaluate the transit drive.

"Why don't we transit from here to the belt? It would save a lot of time." Ryan said.

"We can't do that," Lucy turned to face him.

"Why not?"

"It's the nature of the transit drive," she explained. "Everything connected to the ship is included in the transit. Since we're sitting in this maintenance yard, the ship, and everything connected to it—the maintenance yard and the Earth itself—will become one entity. And as such will all be part of the transit. We would transit the whole planet. Or more likely we'd blow out the drive."

"You're kidding," Ryan said.

"Nope," Lucy replied.

"Ryan," Bove said, "Status?"

"Ready for departure, just say the word," he replied.

"Anyone have issues?" Everyone was ready. "Lockdown." Bove said, "Ready for departure in ten, nine…"

Ryan started the engines sending a soft hum through the ship followed by a slight vibration throughout, typical for a starship. Things would calm once outside the atmosphere in the emptiness of space.

"All systems functioning at optimum capacity," Lucy said.

"Cargo stable," Dan added.

"Departure," Ryan said and pressed the controls to lift them vertically before engaging the engines to send it into orbit. Once they were a thousand meters above the maintenance yard Ryan fired the main engines. The pressure pushed everyone back in their chairs as the velocity increased, the ship vibrated as it split the air while gaining speed. Bove held tight to the arms of the chair until they reached orbit where a sudden loss of gravity released the pressure, and everyone floated in their chairs kept from drifting around the bridge by their restraints.

Lucy switched on the artificial gravity, and everyone settled back into their seats with a sigh of relief. "All systems stable," she said.

"Good," Bove ran his hand over the right arm controls verifying the status, "Let's try out the sensors. Lucy, check what we can pick up around the system. Jack set a course for the asteroid belt, when we get there, we're going to blow a few rocks to pieces. Then we'll head out of the system where we can test the transit drive."

The crew responded to Bove's requests and the ship's speed increased rapidly to one thirty-second light speed heading for the asteroid belt which would be in sight by morning. After running more diagnostics and verifying all systems were functioning correctly, they retired for the night. The next morning, they approached the asteroids, and everyone reported to their stations.

"I have a lock on several asteroids with the sensors. Any one of them can be a target." Lucy turned toward Bove with a broad smile on her face. "These sensors are so much better than the old ones," she said. "I can even pick up rocks in the Kuiper belt as clearly as if we were next to them."

"Weapons ready," Dan said.

"Can you target anything yet?" Bove asked.

"Yeah, rocks in the belt. I can probably hit a few."

"Okay, let's see what happens."

Dan locked the forward laser on one asteroid and the top laser on another, "Ready when you are," he said.

"Let's do it. Fire."

Dan fired each laser hitting both asteroids and blowing them to pieces. "Targets destroyed," he said.

"Impressive," Ryan said.

"Systems status?" Bove asked Lucy.

"Everything's good," she answered.

"Jack, change course to a vertical departure from the system and let me know when we're two million kilometers off the orbital plane."

"Will do," Jack said.

The test flight continued with a transit to Alpha-Centauri and back. Another couple of asteroids were destroyed and the sensors picked up the pieces after each blast. Overall, the test was a great success, and everyone was all smiles as they returned to the maintenance yard and settled in the landing bay.

The bridge cleared except for Bove who remained checking the controls in the captain's chair. Lucy turned towards him. "Something's bothering you," she said. "Has been since before we got back."

"It's nothing," Bove tried to quell her concerns.

"No, it's not nothing. You're on edge and that's not going to help anything. You need to get rid of whatever burden you have."

Bove thought for a minute while Lucy studied him. *She's right*, he thought, *I am on edge, and it won't help during this mission.* "I just have a few things on my mind. Nothing to worry yourself about." He placated her, but she wouldn't have it.

"I thought it was Tom, but I don't see any change now that he's gone."

"Yeah, I have been edgy about him. But things will be fine now. Nothing to worry about—nothing at all." He gave her a weak smile.

"You're lying to yourself. Whatever you have on your mind isn't going away until you talk it out."

"What? Are you the ship's counselor?"

"I've helped several of the crew from time to time." She smiled at him. "And I can help you if you want to get rid of your problem."

"It's too personal," Bove tried again the dissuade her, and again she would have none of it.

"Nothing's too personal when it comes to the safety of the ship and its crew. Which includes me," she emphasized. "I'm not leaving until you tell me what's going on." She leaned back in her chair, crossing her arms over her chest.

"You wouldn't believe me if I told you, so you should let it be."

"I can help, whatever it is. And I'll believe you whatever you tell me. You'll be glad to talk it out."

Bove considered her while she sat watching him, then decided to try it. *What can it hurt*, he sank into his chair, *she'll just think I'm crazy and write me off. But why should I care?* "This cannot leave this room, understood?" He looked her in the eye.

She nodded.

"Okay, here goes." He told her about his vision on Kryth which showed the destruction of their civilization. Then the vision of the three hills where he was redeemed for not stopping the colonization of Kryth. He explained how his broken bones had healed after the three hills vision. And the threat of being left in the bog if he did not help Stella. Then he told her about the latest vision telling him he must intervene to keep a conflict from occurring. When he finished Lucy sat silent for a couple of minutes.

"You think they're dreams?" She asked.

"I've thought about all kinds of possibilities, and nothing makes sense."

"Well, something has to. Once you've eliminated everything it can't be, you'll be left with the thing it is. Didn't Einstein say that?"

"How can bones heal in a single day?"

"Well. They can't. So, it must have been more like six weeks. That's how long it takes for a broken bone to heal."

"I know. But when I woke it was the day after I entered the infirmary, the next day. Explain that."

"Well, I can't. At least not right now. Let me think on it for a couple of days and see what I can come up with."

"Just remember this is not to leave the bridge. You can't tell anyone."

"Yeah, I know."

"Okay, let me know if you have any brilliant ideas."

Lucy nodded and left him alone with his thoughts. And he did feel better after dumping it on her. *Maybe she's right.*

# Twelve

Early Monday morning the crew was making sure everything was ready for departure. Dan and Ryan verified the cargo was secure and checked the manifest, although they weren't sure if it was correct since Tom had not turned in an update. The kitchen was stocked with enough provisions to last three months—more than needed they hoped. Fuel stores and ammunition packets were at maximum. The crew had settled into their cabins with all their personal items and were ready for a long trip. The ship was maxed out with everything needed to complete the mission, and the crew was anxious to be on their way.

Their first stop, Ceti-2, was near the border of the Kazon empire and Bove hoped Stella would help them gain insight into the Kazons and ideas about what to trade. That was if she was there and willing to talk to them. She had left quickly when they returned her home, so Bove was unsure of her attitude toward him. In a way, he felt she was glad to be away from them, and that was understandable since she had been held captive and probably would not have survived if Bove had not interfered. And her government was dealing with a revolution, so she had been preoccupied with the state of affairs. He had the impression she held a high position within the government, but then she had been hijacking weapons. So, what was he to think?

Tom's comment that she was his girlfriend had irritated him at the time, but with further consideration, he could see her in that role. It had been a long time since he had a relationship with a woman and Stella had left an impression. So maybe Tom was partly right, but did she have similar feelings? He dared not hope. How would she react to their arrival without any prior notification?

"Bove," Jack interrupted his thoughts, "I have a transit set for Ceti-2. With this new drive, we can transit directly to the planet; no need to spend days traversing the system."

"Set the transit to the edge of the system," Bove replied. "We need to understand the situation before we approach Ceti-2, When we arrive, we'll decide how to proceed." Bove glanced around the bridge, adjusted his safety strap, and said, "Let's get this ship moving. Is everyone ready?"

Upon confirmation, Bove gave the order to ready the engines, "Departure in twenty seconds, everyone secure?"

The ship lifted smoothly from the maintenance yard, and at a height of a thousand meters, Ryan fired the main engines taking them into orbit where Lucy turned on the artificial gravity giving the ship an earthbound feeling.

"Ahh, gravity," Jack said.

"Tell me when you're ready to transit," Bove said.

"Any time," Ryan replied. "Give me the word."

"Do it," Bove said.

As with any *transit*, there's an instant of pain—less than a hundredth of a second—followed by an instant of confusion. A disorientation where the *transitee* does not know where they are. Then it passes, but in that instant, the *transit* vessel is highly vulnerable. That's why sensors are so important. With sensors of the highest quality danger can be detected and evasive action taken automatically. But there's always the chance an enemy can gain advanced knowledge of transit and be ready to attack when the ship drops into normal space. Even with the best sensors a ship could be unprepared and damaged or destroyed. There's always a risk.

*       *       *

The Ceti system had six planets with only the second and third habitable. The third, although habitable, had an atmosphere of too little oxygen and would need terraforming to make the air breathable. The second was their target and from their position on the outer rim, their cameras could not pick up anything, but their sensors were able to scan the entire system for life signs or ships. Once Bove was satisfied there was no threat lurking between them and Ceti-2 he gave the order to go ahead with small transits from planet to planet. After each, they stopped and rechecked the area. Since many of the first colonies were unfriendly to Earth, he felt he could not be too careful entering a system without prior notification.

When they reached the third planet and settled into an orbit around its moon, they were able to see Ceti-2. It loomed on the viewing screen, a bright blue orb partially covered with clouds. One of its two moons was visible to its left lighting the night side of the planet. A security ring consisting of docking stations circled the planet spaced seven thousand kilometers apart, easily within sight of each other. Each station had six docking bays, and each was well-armed with blasters, cannons, and lasers capable of taking out a star cruiser or larger ship. The ring was impressive not only for its size but for the protection it gave the planet.

Bove remembered being there with trepidation after almost being detained at one of its docking bays when returning Stella. The rebels that held the ring tried to make Bove dock for boarding, but Stella realized what was going on and had them reverse out of the docking bay only to be chased to the southern pole of the planet where they were able to land safely. It was a tense time until the Ibex was out of Ceti-2 space and, on their way back to Sol. As Bove remembered, Stella had abruptly left the ship and disappeared into a nearby building after telling him they should leave as soon as the weapons were unloaded. She did not explain, but she made sure they were well compensated by having one hundred thousand credits deposited in each of their accounts. The credits they had used to upgrade the ship.

"Lucy, send a message," Bove said. "Tell Stella we would like to meet with her to discuss our mission."

"Is that it?" Lucy asked.

"Well, identify us, then we'll see what kind of a response we get."

"Okay," Lucy said rolling her eyes as she sent the message. Within a minute a response came, and Lucy read it, "She says we're welcome to proceed to the security ring for clearance and she'll meet us once we've landed."

"Very good," Bove smiled. the things he remembered about Stella were her fortitude, honesty, and of course her warm smile. He was anxious to see her again. "Take us to the security ring," he said to Ryan. "Dan, stand by in case of any issues, and Lucy monitor their communications. I don't want any surprises."

Acknowledgments came from the crew as Jack laid a course to the security ring and Ryan guided them there at sub-light speed which was fast enough to close the distance between the two planets within minutes. Bove watched as the ship rapidly approached Ceti-2. And shortly they sent a message requesting to dock. An approval came back directing them to station four, docking bay three. Ryan guided the ship cleanly into the bay and the docking clamps closed on the Ibex securing it. An all-clear message came through as a connecting tunnel clamped onto the Ibex's airlock.

"Let's see what we're getting into," Bove said releasing his harness. Ryan stood up from the pilot's seat, Dan, Lucy, and Jack stood to follow Bove to the lift, but Bove stopped them. "Dan, you and Ryan stay here. Keep the ship ready. Jack and Lucy, you're with me." Then they headed down to the airlock on deck six.

The airlock door slid open to reveal three guards waiting. The center guard raised his hand palm facing Bove and his crew, "The captain is all that's needed for clearance," he said.

"Very well," Bove turned to Jack and Lucy. "It'll be fine. Return to the bridge and prepare to take us down." He turned back to the guard, "Okay, what do you need."

The three guards took Bove to a clearing area where they checked his papers, asked how long he would be staying, and his intentions while on the planet. Bove explained he would be meeting with Stella Thorne for a friendly visit, the guard looked up in surprise, "Ms. Thorne?" He asked. Bove nodded. The guard stepped out of the room and quickly returned. He gave Bove full clearance and apologized for the delay. He handed Bove the coordinates of the capital city and instructions for landing at their spaceport, including the landing platform they were to use on arrival. Then apologized again while escorting Bove back to the Ibex. "Enjoy your stay," he said as Bove entered the ship.

"That was strange," Bove said as he settled into the captain's chair.

"What?" Lucy asked.

"The clearance procedure. When I told them we were to visit Stella they checked and quickly cleared me, apologized, gave me directions to the capital, and escorted me back here. They acted like they had done something wrong and didn't want me to realize it. Strange, huh?"

"I guess," Lucy answered turning back to her console.

Bove supplied the coordinates to Jack for the landing pad in the capital city.

"Our landing is set," Jack said.

"Ready to take us down," Ryan said.

"Do it," Bove instructed them.

Ryan backed the Ibex out of the docking bay and headed for the surface. They entered the atmosphere with a jolt that shook the ship. It was a bumpy ride until they had slowed enough to switch to thrusters. On the main view screen, a vast blue orb appeared showing almost half the planet. Part of the major ocean spread along the left side, and the land mass filled the rest of the screen. Jack zoomed in closer to their destination bringing into focus a large city.

The outskirts appeared to be residential dwellings with highways feeding into the city's core where towering buildings were the primary structures making an impressive skyline, not fully appreciated from high above. The descent smoothed out making the view steady revealing more detail of the city. The core featured the tallest buildings and was set off from the rest of the city with a circle of parks.

The ship settled onto the designated landing pad at the capital spaceport on the outer edge of the city away from most of the buildings. Ryan shut down the engines. The crew prepared to leave when Bove stopped them, "I'll go first and see what the reception's like. Wait for my signal." They grumbled but settled back in their seats waiting for instructions.

At the airlock, Bove hesitated, unsure of his approach, then decided to follow Stella's lead. If she is receptive and friendly, he will be the same. But if she doesn't want anything to do with them, he will need to somehow convince her to help them. *I guess either way I'll need to be friendly...* He pressed the button and waited while the door slid open. He stepped out onto the ramp and before him was an array of landing pads, some with ships sitting quietly while others were empty. The roar of engines rumbled across the open space as other ships descended onto their designated spaces. The air was still with the smell of exhaust and tarmac although it was warm. Standing no more than two meters from the ramp's end was Stella, she wore a pair of black slacks, matching boots, and a teal button-up top, open at the neck. A gold chain held a blue stone at her throat, matching earrings adorned her ears, and her light auburn hair hung loose in curls around her neck and shoulders. Her lips were rosy soft and pressed together in a straight line.

Bove looked into her dark eyes, giving her face a stern and serious cast. He paused hoping for some sign of her mood and unsure of what to do. He smiled and raised his hand in greeting.

# Thirteen

Tom stood on the walkway of the Eternia Spaceport in Aeris, the capital city of Anteros, a first colony. Aeris was a busy spaceport and travelers swarmed past Tom on their way to and from flights. The night was hot and sticky with the smells of sweat, tobacco, and bad breath assaulting his senses. He needed a break, a cool drink, someplace quiet where he could think through his next step. The AutoCab glided to a stop in front of him and announced *Pickup for Thomas Edwards*. As he settled into the rear seat the AutoCab said, *State your destination.* "The nearest bar," Tom said and paid the charge.

He had come to Anteros because there were trading ships leaving almost every day and he wanted to get work on one of them. While with Lucus he had been good at managing cargo and weapons and knew he would be able to find work quickly. His credits were in his account just as Bove said so he had finances to cover costs, but he needed work to keep himself stable and out of trouble. He knew from his past experiences if he didn't stay occupied, he would drift into a bad situation just as he had in the past. Before joining Lucus he had started gambling and found himself deep in debt to a loan shark. Lucus helped him settle his debt but that tied him to the Ibex until the loan was satisfied. It had taken three years, and he didn't want to return to that situation again. He hoped his information about work here was correct, if not there was one other colony he could try.

The cab stopped in front of a local bar and announced their arrival. He stepped out and went in. It was busy. Music played loudly and clients crowded the bar and filled the tables. Smoke clouded the air, and the smell of beer and whisky assaulted his nostrils. He coughed and spotted an empty stool toward the end of the bar. As he made his way towards it someone grabbed his shoulder turning him around.

"Well, well, look what we have here." The man's grip tightened on Tom's shoulder, and he reached up with his other hand pulling Tom towards him by his shirt.

"What the hell!" Tom exclaimed, pushing away but the man's grip was tight.

"Don't you remember me?" He stared into Tom's eyes.

Recognition flooded Tom's mind. "You were on the ship," Tom fumbled with his words, "when Zabi boarded us."

"Yeah, and you shot me. Luke, remember?"

"Uh, yeah…" Fear and anger pushed at Tom's mind. *What if Zabi's here,* he thought. *Or more of the crew.* He had to get away, not only from Luke but from the bar too. He felt two large hands grip him from behind.

"What'd you find, Luke?" Zabi said over Tom's shoulder.

Luke pushed Tom around to face Zabi, "This," he said.

Zabi looked down at Tom, "I remember you," he growled. "You shot Luke here. Ain't that right?" Zabi's six-foot-five-inch frame towered four inches over Tom, "What's your name?"

"Tom," Tom answered trying to keep his voice steady.

"Al," Zabi waved over Tom's head, "Help Luke with Tom, our guest. We're heading out."

Al grabbed Tom's upper arm and pulled him along as they headed for the door. *Oh, shit*, Tom struggled, *I'm screwed!* "Where're you taking me?" He tried to break their grip, but they firmly forced him along behind Zabi.

"With us," Zabi answered and led them out the door into the street. A large AutoCab cruised to a stop in front of them and the rear door opened. Luke and Al shoved Tom in and climbed in after him. Zabi slid into the front seat. "To the Dark Star," Zabi stated, and the AutoCab was off.

It only took a couple of minutes to arrive at the Dark Star and a couple more to haul Tom into it and deposit him in the brig. *Great!* Tom thought as the force field flickered to life.

Twenty minutes later the field blanked out. "Come with me," the man said.

"Where to?" Tom asked.

"Follow me."

Tom followed down a couple of corridors up two levels and into a room where Zabi sat at the head of a small table. "Thank you, Samuel," he said. Then to Tom, "Have a seat."

Tom sat, the muscles across his shoulders tightened, his hands gripped the arms of the chair, and sweat trickled down his spine. He took a deep breath.

"Well, what am I to do with you?" Zabi glared at him. "Send you out the airlock, hum?" He watched Tom squirm, "Are you here to spy on us? Are you setting us up for that sleazy colleague of yours—the one that forced us off your ship? Just why are you here?"

"You brought me here," Tom said. "I was minding my own business when you hauled me off. And I'm not spying on anyone, I'm looking for work."

"Well, lucky you. This ship needs cleaning, and it looks like you're just the man for the job. You're hired. Ruby will show you what to do." Zabi turned to the console behind him and pressed a button, "Ruby! Front and center!" He yelled.

Seconds later Ruby came in, "Yeah?"

"We have a new hand to clean the ship. Show him what to do and keep a tight rein on him so he doesn't cause any trouble." Turning to Tom he added, "I use the airlock to drop trash, and when there's trouble, I consider the cause trash. You get my drift?"

Tom nodded and followed Ruby out into the corridor. "You're going to start on the bridge where I can keep an eye on you. Follow me."

The bridge was similar to the bridge of the Ibex And the crew was busy at the consoles along the sides. Ruby gave Tom orders for cleaning. He was to get every detail sparkling. She wanted the bridge spotless in the next six hours. Tom buckled down and started cleaning while trying to figure a way out of this mess. He considered making a run for it at the first chance he got but reconsidered that possibility when he heard they were lifting off in a matter of minutes. Then he considered stealing a shuttle and making a break for it. *Would they shoot one of their shuttles?* He wondered. Then decided that wasn't workable. He could try to make a break for it at the next stop. Maybe they would leave him alone for a while, long enough to slip away, doubtful. He continued cleaning, slowly losing hope of escape.

Zabi appeared on the bridge and took his seat in the captain's chair.

"Where to?" Carter asked.

"Is the cargo loaded?" Zabi asked Ruby.

"Yes, sir," she replied, "Loaded and secure. We can leave when you're ready."

"Mila, what's the ship's status?"

"Everything's in prime order, she's as good as new."

"Hear that, Tom," Zabi said making Tom raise his head to look at him. "It took us three weeks to get the ship back in shape after your boss, or whoever he is, destroyed our systems with that pathetic ship of yours. If I ever see it again, I'm going to blow it to hell," He glared at Tom like he wanted to blow Tom to hell. "Too bad you won't be able to tell that SOB my intentions."

"Yeah, too bad," Tom answered. 'Just to be clear, I had nothing to do with shooting your ship."

"You shot my crew!" Zabi's voice filled the bridge. "Same difference. And you are going to pay the same price, you got that?" Zabi glared at Tom, "So, don't give me any lip, our ship doesn't need cleaning that bad." He turned away from Tom and said, "Everything ready?" to no one in particular.

"Where to?" Carter asked again.

"Get us out of this system while I figure out our next stop," Zabi stood and glared at Tom as he left the bridge.

"Yes, sir," Carter said to his back.

Tom let out a breath of relief. *I have got to figure a way off this ship*. He was sure they would throw him out of the airlock if he made one wrong move or comment. *Best to keep quiet*, he went back to cleaning, still trying to find a way to escape.

# Fourteen

"So, you're back," Stella's voice was flat and serious. A light breeze ruffled her hair across her face. She pushed it away from her eyes with the back of her hand. "Was the reward not enough?" She asked.

With tight lips, Bove made another attempt to smile which failed miserably. "No, the reward was more than enough. We…"

"Then why are you here?" She interrupted, arms akimbo, legs apart. She looked delightful and deadly serious.

Bove flushed at the thought. "Well, I wanted to get some advice. I thought you might help, but clearly, you're not happy to see me. Maybe this was a mistake." He turned to board the ship, then turned back to Stella, "It was nice to see you again," he said.

"Advice, huh?" She stopped him.

'Yeah," he turned back wanting to see a smile, but kept his face blank trying not to show his disappointment.

"What do you need advice about?" her face softened.

"It's about the Kazons. I have…"

"The Kazons? What do you have to do with them?' She glanced over her shoulder like she was expecting someone, then turned back with concern etched on her face.

"Nothing, I have a mission to get information." Bove held up a hand to stop Stella from protesting. "Let me explain."

"Not here," she said, then before Bove could respond she continued, "How big's your crew? And is Tom with you?"

Bove shook his head at the change of subject, "There's four, plus me, and no, Tom's not with us."

"Good to hear. What happened?" She asked.

"He decided to go his own way."

"That leaves you a bit short-handed." She paused and looked Bove straight in the eyes, and the corner of her mouth twitched up. "Tell your crew to come along, I'll get some refreshments and they can relax a bit." She turned toward the entrance, "Follow me," she glanced back to see that he was coming.

Bove tapped his communicator, "Jack, get everyone and join me."

As he headed after Stella the crew came out hurrying to catch up to him. Stella led them into the main building, across to the exit, and into an AutoCab which lifted straight up higher than the tallest buildings making the view of the city uninterrupted. From outside the city, the skyline was in sharp relief against the clear blue sky and resembled a mountain range with low buildings like foothills rising to the peaks in the city center. It was fabulous.

The AutoCab was above all other vehicles and flew uninterrupted straight into the city center where it stopped and descended until they came to a stop in front of one of the towering buildings in a sprawling complex.

"This is our seat of government," Stella said. We can talk here." She herded them into a conference room in a smaller building. The room was dominated by a table and six chairs. There were two pictures of flowers on the end walls and a picture window overlooking a small garden. "There's a lounge across the hall if anyone would like to relax a bit." She added then disappeared out the door.

"Well," Jack said looking around. "That was quick."

"I think I'll go to the lounge," Dan headed out the door followed by Ryan.

"You think she'll help," Lucy asked.

Before anyone could answer Stella came back followed by two men dressed in casual slacks and shirts. They took seats at the table, "This is Anthan Nostov – Head of Ceti-2 security, and this is Kator Hismith – Minister of Foreign Affairs. They will take part in this discussion." Stella took a seat at the head of the table extending her arm towards the remaining seats.

Jack glanced around at the three empty chairs, "Well,' he said, "I could use a break. You want to join me?" He asked Lucy.

She pulled out a chair and sat, "I'm staying."

Bove looked at Anthan Nostov and Kator Hismith, "Nice to meet you," he hesitated, glanced at Stella and Lucy, then took a seat.

Jack left for the lounge.

"So," Stella said, "what is this about?"

Bove nodded, "We have a mission to gather information about the Kazons."

"What kind?" Kator asked.

Bove turned to him, "The Kazons have claimed Kryth, the Delta planet of Pheonix-Gamma, is in their territory, and…"

"Is it?" Anthan interrupted.

"We've had a colony there for the last six months and they're getting well established. The president doesn't want them moved just because the Kazons claim the planet's theirs. Their message was fairly strict and threatening. And now our government wants more information about them to know how to respond to their claim. We have been tasked with gathering that information, so I am here to see if you have any insights that could help our mission."

"You didn't answer my question. Does the planet belong to them?" Anthan asked again.

Bove looked at him, "No, it's not within their territory."

"Do they have reason to claim it?" Not waiting for an answer Anthan continued, "We don't help if there's any reason, any valid reason for the Kazons to be claiming it. So, are you sure Earth has the right to the colony?"

"I was with the team to verify the planet was suitable for colonization. We found ruins from an earlier colony, a human colony from Earth, and no evidence of Kazon influence. So, yes, I am sure they have no claim to it." Bove's voice rose a bit as he felt pressured to justify Earth's claim to Kryth, and then he added, "It's well outside Kazon territory."

"Good," Anthan said, "But we need to verify your information." He tapped a communicator in his ear and instructed whoever was on the other end to verify Bove's information.

"What kind of information are you looking for?" Kator asked.

Bove considered his question for a moment and rubbed his brow. "The Kazons threatened to remove the colonists if we don't, and our government wants to know if they can. We are to find out how much of a threat they are."

"Our government?" Anthan gave Bove a look that could kill. "We are not governed by Earth." He said flatly. "Let's not confuse things."

"Of course," Bove was suddenly unsure of what his standing was. "I didn't mean to include you in that statement, only me and my crew."

Anthan nodded, but Bove wasn't sure if that was a nod of understanding or clarification. Anthan tapped his ear, "It seems your information is correct. The Kazons have no rights to Kryth."

"How do you plan on getting that information?" Kator asked.

Bove nodded to Anthan, then said to Kator, "We plan to find something they want or need. Something we can trade with them. That way we can get close enough to ask questions and get the information we need."

"That's not going to work," Stella said. "They're very selective about who they trade with, and if they don't know you, they're not apt to make a deal."

"Even if we have what they need?"

"Even if you have what they need."

"But," Kator interrupted, "I believe there are some items rare enough to entice them."

"Like what?" Bove turned to Kator.

"Cesium," Kator glanced at Stella then back to Bove. "They don't have any on their home world."

"What's it used for?" Bove leaned forward.

"Propulsion, for missiles and ships."

"Don't they have transit drives?" Bove raised his eyebrows in wonder.

"They do, but cesium is used for short-range ships and missiles. Why use a transit drive for ships that patrol locally, or are used for close-range fighting like deployment from a star cruiser?"

"I see your point," Bove said.

"That doesn't sound good," Lucy folded her arms over her chest. "Should we be helping arm them?"

"Probably not, but do we have a choice?" Bove leaned back in his chair, "Where would we find some?"

"Sancus," Anthan said.

"And that may be a problem for you," Stella added.

"Problem? Why?" Bove asked.

"They're very anti-Earth because of the way Earth treated them. After they set up their first city, Earth canceled shipments citing a lack of funds and supplies, which was a total fabrication. They had plenty of supplies and funds for other colonies. Why they chose to stop shipments to Sancus is unknown. But that left Sancus disillusioned with Earth."

"They still feel that way?" Lucy asked. "It's been a hundred years…"

"Hate runs deep," Stella said. "Look at your own history. There was animosity toward foreigners, different religions, different sexual orientations, and even different skin color in many countries for hundreds of years. It has only been recently that it's started to abate."

"I guess that's true," Lucy conceded. "Still, it's not good for us."

"No, it's not," Stella agreed, "you're not going to be welcome when you go there."

Bove glanced around the table, "We'll have to deal with that once we get there. Do you have its location?"

Stella nodded, then glanced at Anthan and Kator, "Give us a minute, please," she said to Bove.

"Sure," Bove motioned to Lucy, and they left for the lounge.

Jack, Ryan, and Dan were at a table alone and away from everyone else there. Bove and Lucy joined them.

"So," Dan asked, "did they give you anything useful?"

"They doubt we will learn anything. They said if they don't know us, they likely won't trade with us."

"Did they have any suggestions?" Jack asked.

Bove filled them in about the cesium and Sancus and before anyone could ask a question, Stella came in and settled herself in the soft chair, "So,' she started, "I'll come with you to Sancus to act as an intermediary. The Sancusians will be more likely to talk with me than you. If it's acceptable with you of course,"

"How hostile are they," Dan asked.

"They might kill you as soon as talk with you, that is if they let you land. They could shoot you down if they know you're from Earth. With my help, we can avoid that."

"They're okay with you?" Bove asked.

Stella nodded.

Bove glanced at everyone, "I say we take her with us."

'Fine by me," Jack answered. Lucy and Ryan agreed, but Dan hesitated and then reluctantly agreed.

"Okay," Bove smiled. "You're coming along." Then he added, "I think you know everyone except Ryan. He's our new pilot and medic.'

"And I understand Tom's gone," Stella glanced around at the crew.

'That's right," Jack said flatly.

"That will make things easier," Stella was visually relieved. Tom had been in charge of her while she was held for turnover to Zabi. And he had only tolerated her after they received the reward credits. Changing the subject, she asked, 'When do we leave?"

"We'll be on our way as soon as you're ready," Bove told her. "We can meet you at the ship. Just show us how to get back to it."

Stella tapped her communicator and gave instructions to take them back to their ship, "I'll join you shortly," she smiled at Bove.

Bove felt a shiver run through him, he opened his mouth to say something, but nothing came out. He tried to turn his open mouth into a smile and hoped for the vest.

*       *       *

Bove was waiting at the airlock when Stella arrived and accompanied her to the crew quarters on deck three. "These three are empty," he said waving his arm towards the available cabins, "take your pick."

Stella looked at them and then selected the one she had hidden in the last time she was aboard the ship. "This one will do fine."

Bove watched her enter and drop her things on the bunk. She looked around briefly then turned to Bove and waited.

"Uh," Bove stammered, "Is it okay?" When she didn't say anything, he continued, "Do you think the Sancusians will be that unwelcoming?"

"Why else would I come?"

"I don't know, fun?" He looked down at his feet feeling foolish. *Of course, she thought they would be difficult and that's why she's coming, to help us. Nothing to do with me.* He looked up, took a breath, and said, "I didn't mean that. I just thought you might have other reasons to come with us."

"Like what?"

"I don't know, I shouldn't have said anything." He shifted his feet and crossed his arms over his chest, unfolded his arms, and leaned against the doorframe. "I was just wondering why you would want to help us."

"Well,' she said, "you did me a favor and I felt I owed you something, so I offered to come. That's all. And, of course, you don't know what you're headed for."

"Then tell me."

"Shouldn't the crew hear about it too and know what they're getting into?"

"Yeah, they should," he paused. "So," he continued, "when this is done do want to be left back on Ceti-2?"

"When this is done, we'll see."

"Meaning?"

"We'll see," she glanced over Bove's head into the corridor.

Bove pushed away from the wall trying to compose himself, he took a breath and said, "We'll have a briefing when we're on our way." he backed into the corridor, "Come to the bridge when you're ready. We'll be leaving shortly." He left her standing in her cabin. And as he entered the lift, he hoped he hadn't made a complete fool of himself by suggesting she was here for anything other than helping them.

# Fifteen

The Dark Star came to a stop at the farthest edge of the Anteras system after a five-day journey. Zabi didn't trust Tom or like the idea of keeping him around. He thought it was a setup for Bove, although Zabi didn't know Bove's name he wanted more information about him, and Tom was the way to get it. He felt sure with the right encouragement Tom would spill, then Luke could get the revenge he was so anxious to have.

"Ruby," Zabi shouted into the ship's communication terminal, "bring Tom to my office."

"On my way," Ruby responded.

Zabi sat down behind the desk in his office. It was a small room with a desk, a couple of cabinets built into the walls, and a couple of chairs bolted to the floor and facing the desk. There were no decorations on the walls and a computer terminal on the desk that could be lowered into the surface, leaving the desk clear, now it was raised and glowing uselessly.

Ruby knocked lightly then slid the door aside and peeked in. "I have Tom," she said.

"Bring him in," Zabi ordered.

Ruby pushed Tom through the doorway and waited, her hand keeping the door from sliding closed.

"That'll be all," Zabi told her. She vanished, letting the door slide quietly shut.

Tom trembled and shuffled from foot to foot. Fear covered his face in beads of sweat.

"Sit," Zabi said. "How are you getting along?"

'I…" Tom started to reply.

"No matter," Zabi interrupted. "I have been considering what to do with you. Luke thinks the airlock is too quick, what do you think? Never mind, I agree with him. There are better ways to make you pay. One of my favorites is piecemeal. You know what that is?

Tom shook his head, sweat trickled down his forehead, and his voice caught in his throat. He coughed.

"Yeah, I thought so." Zabi withdrew a long sharp knife and pointed it at Tom. "Piecemeal is where I dispose of you piece by piece. It's very messy, so I don't do it here. I don't like to get my office dirty. You know what I mean?" Zabi put his knife away, "We'll deal with you shortly." He switched on his communicator. "Luke, come to my office."

"On my way," Luke answered.

Tom took a deep breath trying to steady himself. Trying to think things through. "Zabi," he started. Zabi looked at him. "Uh, do you really want me? Or do you want Bove?"

"Bove? Who's that?"

"He's the guy that took your weapons. The guy that threw you off the Ibex. The guy that kept us from turning over the woman."

"Bove? That's his name? He disabled my ship!" Zabi slammed his hand on his desk.

"Yeah," Tom agreed suddenly feeling better.

"Oh, yes, I would love to get him. I'd show him the best time, oh yeah, the best!" Zabi stopped and glared at Tom, "Do you know where he is?"

"I know where he's going." Tom offered.

Luke came in, glanced at Tom then turned to Zabi, "How are we going to do it? Not the airlock, I hope."

"Hold on, Luke," Zabi said. "He may have something here." He pointed to a chair, "Sit. Now, what do you know?" He asked Tom.

"Well," Tom started, then stopped. "How do I know you won't kill me if I tell you what I know?"

Zabi laughed, "Kill you? Who said anything about killing you? Of course, we won't kill you." Then his face blanked, eyes narrowed, and he stroked his beard with his long fingers. "What do you know?"

"Can you assure me you won't kill me?'

"Sure, but will you believe me? It doesn't matter. If your information proves to be of value, I'll let you go. This time." He looked at Luke who was not happy but didn't say anything knowing to object to Zabi's decision could be fatal, so he just sat back.

Tom wiped a hand across his forehead, and took a breath, "Okay," he leaned as far from Luke as he could get. "Bove took a job to gather information about the Kazons. He's going to their home world in the next few weeks. He's planning to trade with them and get the information he needs."

"Who gave him this job?" Zabi asked.

"The government," Tom said.

"Hum, what information are they looking for? And how is Bove going to get it?"

"I don't know. There's a problem with the new colonies on Pheonix-Gamma. Something about the Kazons saying the planet belongs to them. The government wants to know what the Kazons are planning to do about it."

"I see," Zabi said stroking his beard in thought. "You say he's going to be on their home world in the next few weeks? Can you be more specific than that?"

"I don't know any more than that. When I left, they had accepted the offer and were planning to trade with the Kazons. That's all I know."

"That's not much, is it Luke?"

"Nope," Luke agreed.

"But," Zabi continued, "I have been trading with the Kazons for several years. They know me and are always eager to help out. I'm sure they would be more than happy to let me know when he shows up there." Zabi stepped to his bar, "We'll celebrate with a drink," and poured an amber liquid into three glasses and handed one to each of them. "If this pans out you will be free to go," he said to Tom.

Tom let out a slow breath and downed his drink.

"Ruby," Zabi yelled into his communicator, "Come and take Tom out of here."

*       *       *

When he was gone, Zabi looked at Luke, "You're not happy," he said.

"It's fine," Luke said clipping his words.

Zabi knew Luke wanted revenge for being shot and Zabi didn't blame him. Zabi wanted revenge for what Bove did to him and his ship. Bove had disabled his engines and weapons with a ship that was junk. It had taken three weeks to get everything repaired. That angered Zabi more than anything, if the ship had been a match to the Dark Star, Zabi could understand, but the Ibex was a cargo ship in poor repair with no weapons, and it had disabled the Dark Star. If that got out Zabi's reputation would be trashed, and he could not have that.

So far no one had heard anything about the encounter, he guessed the Ibex kept silent about it. Smart move.

"He'll get what he deserves, I promise," Zabi told Luke. "As soon as we have solid information about Bove and his ship, you can have him. Just don't make a mess on my ship."

Luke smiled, "There're ways to do what I want and not leave a mess. As you well know."

"Yeah, I do," Zabi agreed. "Now, as long as he's here I want him cleaning this ship, even the cargo bay."

"I'll see to it." Luke gave Zabi a thumbs-up and left.

# Sixteen

Stella entered the bridge and promptly took a seat in the captain's chair, "You've made some improvements," she said studying the armrest console. "Nice."

"We have," Bove answered her, "It helps to see the ship's status without having to ask."

Stella looked up catching Bove's eye, "I see," she said.

"You can use Tom's chair," Bove pointed to his left at the empty seat next to Dan.

Stella slid out of the captain's chair, sauntered over to Tom's console, and sat down, "Am I in charge of cargo now?"

"You think you can handle it?" Bove sat down and tapped a couple of buttons on the armrest, "Status," he said.

Jack, Ryan, Dan, and Lucy all went through their checklist verifying everything was good to go and gave Bove the all-clear. "Cargo?" He asked Stella.

She looked down at the console, touched a couple of pads, nodded to herself, and then looked up at Bove, "Everything's secure," she said.

Two minutes later they were lifting off Ceti-2 on their way to Sancus.

*       *       *

In the Conference room on deck two, Stella sat at the end of the table facing Bove. To Bove's right were Jack and Lucy and to his left sat Ryan and Dan. Bove glanced around the table and then to Ryan and said, "Did anyone bring you up to speed concerning Stella?"

Ryan nodded, 'Yeah, Jack told me about what happened."

"Okay," Bove turned to Stella and asked, "So, what do you know about Sancus?"

Stella glanced around the table considering her reply. "They're an original colony established several years before Ceti-2 during the first colonization," she took a breath and continued. "They had settled in two locations and were doing very well when Earth decided to stop shipments to them. Earth said they should be able to support themselves. What Earth didn't understand was how difficult it was to get anything started on Sancus, much less keep it stable and growing. They needed those supplies and without them over half the population died within a year. Sancus didn't forgive Earth and after they stabilized, they cut off all contact, and still hold to that. So, anyone from Earth going there will not sit well. You're heading into an angry hornet's nest and may not come out in one piece."

"And they'll talk to you?"

"Yeah, we also lost support from Earth and prefer not to deal with them."

"Then why help us?" Jack asked.

"Well, like I told Bove, you did me a favor, so I feel I owe you one." Stella paused, looking down at her hands folded in her lap. She shrugged her shoulders and looked up at Bove, "I consider you a friend."

"I only did the right thing." Bove said, "Anyone would have done the same." He wasn't sure that was true, but he didn't want special treatment because of it.

Yet, he liked hearing Stella say that, even though he wished for more. Friends were something he hadn't had in a long time and a companion even longer, he was still in college when he last had a female companion, and after joining the GPF he lost contact with everyone except his parents. The GPF didn't encourage companionship and kept the agents mixed up so no bonds could develop. Then when his parents died, he was alone.

Now, with the crew he still felt he could not be friends with any of them, it might jeopardize his authority on the ship. But since Stella was not part of the crew, he felt comfortable letting her get close to him.

"So," Lucy said, "how are you going to help us?"

Stella turned to face her, "When we arrive at Sancus I will do all the talking," she said.

"I'm the one that needs the cesium," Bove reminded her. "Shouldn't I negotiate?"

"If they find out you're from Earth they'll shut down. You'll get nothing. In fact, you might not be lucky enough to get off their planet."

"It's that bad?" Dan's face blanched. "I thought the Kazons were bad."

"Yes, it is," Stella said. "So, Bove, you will pose as part of my crew and say nothing. I will negotiate a deal for the cesium."

"You'll need to get up to date on our cargo," Jack added. "You should know about everything we have on board."

"Are there logs?" Stella asked, looking at Dan.

"Mmmm, I'll see if I can find them. Tom kept everything to himself, but I'm sure they'll be easy enough to locate."

"Okay, do it and give them to Stella," Bove leaned forward resting his arms on the table and looking at Stella, "We'll transit in two days so use the time to learn everything you can." Then he turned his attention to the crew, "Anything else?"

When no one responded he dismissed them.

The crew talked quietly as they filed out.

Stella stood when the room was empty, and said, "Don't take this lightly," then left.

"Never," Bove mumbled to the empty room.

*     *     *

Sancus was the third of six planets circling the star Nexrima. Ibex arrived outside the farthest planet and set velocity to one thirty-second light speed. They would reach Sancus in four days. It was Stella's suggestion they go in slow; it would give her a chance to assess the situation. It had been more than two years since she had contact with them, so caution was the prudent choice. Bove had complained, but he came around after Stella pointed out her superior knowledge of the situation.

During the four days of travel, Stella could learn about the cargo in the hold, so Bove took her down to deck six to review the manifest and learn about it. "This brings back bad memories," she said as they stepped into the hold. She had been held in one of the pens while on the ship waiting to be turned over to Zabi. "I'd rather be anywhere else on the ship," she said, "but I guess we need to do this."

"I think it will help." Bove had noticed how nervous she had been heading down to the hold and guessed it was from her captivity; memories can be forceful and very real. She had to learn about the cargo and the only way was to check the hold. Bove would try to make it as pleasant as possible. "We're going to check the inventory against the manifest, so focus to keep your mind off things."

"Off things?" She almost laughed, "It'll never happen." She stopped at the entrance to the hold and scanned the area, "Any of them could be my cage," her voice was low, almost a whisper.

"We can start in the holding area. Then wander through the cargo as we review it."

She nodded, still unsure how she felt about spending any time in the cargo bay. But once in the holding area, her tension lessened.

Bove produced a list of the cargo, "Ok," he said. "Let's see what you know."

"Let's," she half smiled and wrapped her arms around herself as if she were cold.

Each day of the journey they spend three hours verifying the cargo. He went into each pen and called out the contents of the containers while she checked off the items on the list. In the end, she knew as much about the cargo as Tom had and was no longer hesitant about being in the hold.

*       *       *

Bove settled in the captain's chair while Stella took Tom's place. As they approached Sancus, they were hailed, "State your affiliation and purpose," the voice said.

"You're up," Bove switched communications to Stella.

"This is the Ibex," Stella said. "We're based on Ceti-2, a first colony and we wish to develop a trading agreement with Sancus."

"Hold in orbit," came the reply.

"Acknowledged," Stella answered.

"Establish orbit," Bove told Ryan who did at once.

The bridge fell silent. Stella shifted in her chair. Minutes passed.

The silence broke, "You have permission to land. Directions have been sent to your navigation system. If you deviate from these directions, you will be fired on. Is that clear?"

"Acknowledged," Stella replied.

"We'll take the shuttle down," Bove stated to no one in particular.

"I'll meet you there," Stella stood and left the bridge.

"Transfer the directions to shuttle one," Bove told Jack who nodded. "You're in charge while I'm gone."

The descent took less than thirty minutes, and once the shuttle was secure on the landing pad, Bove cut the engine.

"Okay," he said, "Let's see what's out there to greet us." Before moving he switched communications to the Ibex, "Be prepared to break orbit and transit on my order. Even if we aren't back, understood?"

Jack's voice was calm, but his words were unsure, "Uh… yeah.

Stella stepped off the shuttle followed by Bove. The landing pad was part of a larger spaceport with ten pads in view. Past the landing area were buildings making up the port. Beyond the port were more buildings towering in the distance making up what appeared to be a major city. The sky was clear and the air warm with a slight breeze ruffling Stella's hair.

Two men stood less than two meters from the exit backed by four guards, "Welcome," the man on the right said. "I am Firaaz Kryler, Council Chairman, and this is Zohn Weber, Minister of Foreign Affairs. And you are?"

"Stella Thorne and this is my pilot, Bove Sandle," Stella extended her hand in greeting.

"Very good," Firaaz said ignoring Stella's gesture, "Please follow me" He turned and headed for a transport sitting on the next landing pad. Once loaded into the transport Firaaz said, "We will be going to the Ming complex here in Mingbourne where our administrative offices are."

The transport raced through the city of enormous buildings covering huge areas of land. Unlike cities on Earth, these buildings were single structures sitting on the equivalent of two city blocks. It was all very impressive. The transport flew above all other vehicles in a corridor reserved for government use making the trip go quickly. Shortly they arrived at their destination where Firaaz led them from the transport into a huge building and deposited them in a small room. Firaaz pointed to a cart with refreshments, "Please sit. Refresh yourselves. A drink, perhaps?" He poured drinks for everyone, setting the glasses on the table, as Zohn took a chair opposite Bove and Stella.

Firaaz sat at the head of the table. He glanced at Zohn, then asked, "What can we do for you?"

"We would like to establish a trading agreement with your colony."

"And what would you be trading?" Zohn asked before Stella could continue.

"We have a variety of items for an initial trade and depending on your needs we can provide more."

"And what do you need in return?"

"We are developing some advanced spacecraft that need plasma propulsion engines. And, as I am sure you know, plasma propulsion needs cesium."

"Yes, they do," Firaaz stated. "Do you have a list of your cargo?"

"Certainly, Bove." Bove handed her the display pad and Stella handed it to Firaaz who passed it to Zohn. "This is our current cargo, and from our other trading agreements we will be able to replenish many items on the list."

Zohn perused the list nodding as he scrolled. "You have a good amount of medical equipment I see. Are these the latest technology?" he asked, smiling at Stella.

"Of course. We deal in only the best."

"How much cesium are you looking for?" He asked.

"Four thousand kilos," Stella said. Bove noted the slight look Zohn gave Firaaz.

Looking at Bove, Zohn said, "You're quiet."

Bove shifted in his chair knowing when he spoke, they would know he was from Earth. The very thing they wanted to avoid. But before he opened his mouth to respond, Stella spoke for him, "He's here to fly the shuttle and has no say in this trade agreement. It's best if he stays quiet."

"A little idle talk shouldn't hurt. What do you do on the ship, Bove?" Zohn asked ignoring Stella.

Bove opened his mouth to answer, but Stella raised a hand stopping him. "I would like to settle a trade agreement before any idle talk."

"Strictly business, huh?" Firaaz asked.

"Are you interested in trading?" She countered.

"Can you provide more medical equipment than is in your cargo?" Zohn asked.

"Can you provide our cesium?"

Zohn smiled holding Stella with his eyes for a moment, then Firaaz intruded, "Would you like to visit our cesium mines? I can arrange a tour tomorrow."

Bove felt his shoulders tighten as he watched Zohn's eye glide over Stella. He kept his face blank as his hands curled around the arms of the chair.

"That would be most informative," Stella said turning toward Firaaz with a smile.

It was an unexpected offer and Bove wasn't sure of the reason. He thought he should talk to Stella before going but now was not the time.

"Wonderful," Firaaz smiled back. "We have guest rooms you can use for the night. Of course, we will need to move to another location, but I'm sure you will find the accommodations more than satisfying."

"That's very gracious, but we would prefer to stay on our shuttle. We can inform the crew of our plans for the next day or so. And tend to unfinished business from there."

"As you wish," Firaaz nodded as he stood, "Zohn would you see our guests to their shuttle?"

Zohn smiled at Stella ignoring Bove and saying, "I would love to accompany our guests. Come with me." He held out his hand to Stella, then dropped it to his side when she ignored it.

Bove kept his face blank even though he would like to have smacked Zohn across the face. He stood and followed them out to the transport holding his anger and his mouth closed.

# Seventeen

The Dark Star sat unmoving while Zabi pondered his next move. Tom had given him information that Bove was going to Ardonia supposedly to learn about the Kazon's military status. *What does he think? They'll just tell him?* Zabi shook his head in disbelief. He was sure the Kazons would not talk to him, much less tell him anything of use.

He straightened his legs under the desk in his private office and yawned stretching his arms above his head to relieve the tightness in his shoulders. He had to decide if Tom's info was right, or if he was giving him crap to gain time before his demise. There was no way to know for sure. Yet, if he kept him around until he could verify what Bove was going to do, he could still get rid of him. After all, he wasn't going anywhere.

Zabi leaned back in his chair taking a deep breath to clear his head. He decided to keep Tom, and if it turned out he was lying, well, Tom would wish he could jump out the airlock himself. Zabi would make sure of that.

He pressed the ship's broadcast button to send an announcement throughout the ship. "Crew," he said, "report to the main conference room immediately." He leaned back in his chair, *Telling the Kazons that Bove is a spy will land him in their prison system for the rest of his life*, an evil smile creased his lips, and his fingers curled closed, *Oh yeah.*

Zabi went to the conference room and sat at the head of the table. The crew entered sliding chairs out and sitting down. *They won't be happy about the change of plans*, he watched them settle, *but they will get R&R later after I deal with Bove*. After all, their time off didn't concern him, he only wanted what would benefit him. And getting Bove would benefit his mood tremendously.

"What's this about?" Carter asked.

"Something's come up and we're going to Ardonia." Zabi didn't hold back. His voice was low and there was no disputing it.

"What?" Ruby's face tightened into a frown, "I've made plans."

"Change them," Zabi's forehead creased, and his eyes narrowed. "Besides this will be a short visit and you'll have some time off when we're done." He looked at the rest of the crew for any more complaints. They knew better than to say anything, once Zabi made a decision there was no changing it. They would have to deal with whatever he decided. "So," he said, "Sam, plot a course to Ardonia and prepare for immediate departure.

The crew filed out heading for their stations to prepare for the change of plans. Each grumbled but was too afraid of Zabi to voice their concern. Once on the bridge, Sam set parameters for the Ardonia system while Luke prepared to transit.

"Execute," Zabi said to Luke, and an instant of pain swept through the crew ending in a moment of total confusion. Everyone quickly adjusted to their new location at the outer rim of the Ardonia system near the eighth planet. "Scan the area," Zabi told Mila. "See if there's any ships around."

"Scanning now," she responded. "I'm not picking up anything unusual."

"Carter, send a message to Dengar Kergan that we'll arrive shortly."

"Sam, set a transit to Krycink. Mila, prepare to scan again when we get there."

When they arrived at Ardonia's second moon and scanned, they found nothing unusual. "Contact Dengar and tell him we have vital information concerning their planet Kryth," Zabi switched on the main viewer, and a display of the planet Ardonia appeared on the screen. A large bright blue ball shined in the sun's glare. It had the same proportions of water and land as Earth. Clouds covered parts of the land mass while other areas were clear. Cities were visible dotting the surface with roads connecting them like veins. Ardonia was slightly larger than Earth with a high gravity index causing the Kazons to be shorter but stronger than humans. They were bulky with powerful chests and arm muscles, and legs thicker than human legs. Their cat eyes and fur covering their heads were so unfamiliar it was disturbing, and when they became angry their claws extended into sharp needle-like points giving them an intimidating appearance that was rather scary.

A message came in instructing them to go to a landing pad in the spaceport near the capital city of Arender. Zabi had supplied weapons to the Kazons from time to time to help suppress uprisings, so they knew him and allowed him to land and disembark without a search.

Luke lowered the Dark Star onto the landing pad in the spaceport and when the ship had settled, he shut down the engines. The spaceport was busy with ships from human colonies as well as Earth. Trade with the Kazons was popular and rewarding, particularly for Zabi who had ultramodern weapons.

Having traded with the Kazons for years, Zabi and his crew knew the city and what it had to offer the space weary. There were bars and casinos, a multitude of stores, and other entertainment. Shops that catered to human needs with food and goods.

Zabi motioned Carter to him, "Tell the crew they have shore leave. Everyone needs to be back here in two days by ten PM. We'll be leaving whether they're here or not."

Carter activated the ship-wide communication and sent the message then asked, "What should we do with Tom?"

"Put him in the brig. We'll deal with him when we leave."

"Luke, you're with me," Zabi said as he stood to leave.

"Where are we going," Luke asked.

"We're going to see Dengar Kergan to tell him about Bove's plan to spy on them. I'm going to fix it so he gets arrested. It'll serve him right. In fact, life in prison is too good for him."

"Yeah," Luke nodded in agreement. "Why do that? You could wait out by Krycink for him, to turn up, then destroy his ship and him."

"And if he transits into orbit around Ardonia? We would miss him. No, the best way is to let the Kazons take care of him. They won't tolerate a spy and when he arrives, they'll put him away, probably for life. I would like to be there to see his face when they arrest him. Wouldn't that be stellar?"

"Uh, yeah," Luke nodded.

Their transport arrived to take them to Dengar, the deputy of internal affairs. Dengar dealt with all matters involving trade.

Zabi entered their destination and the transport lifted vertically to an express corridor high above the spaceport and headed for the city. Spreading for miles in every direction the city was breathtaking, towering buildings reached upward as if trying to grasp the transport, and below them, vehicles laced their way through the corridors between the buildings making a maze of moving objects threading their way through the city. The corridors between the buildings looked like canyons crawling with night creatures–dark and forbidding.

The transport slowed and hovered for a moment, then began to rapidly descend. Buildings rushed up at them as the transport approached a landing pad amid the complex making up the seat of the ruling council. After slowing and setting down without even a nudge, the door slid open and Zabi disembarked to be greeted by Aurra Jedex, Dengar's assistant. Aurra wore a comfortable Kazon suit made of light blue fibers, like cotton. His jacket covered a matching shirt buttoned to the neck. He wore blue pants and black boots polished to a high shine. His short facial fur was a light orange covering his head and neck. His height was just under two meters and his build was thick and muscular. He raised a powerful arm with a closed paw and clasped it against his chest as a greeting of welcome. Zabi responded with the same gesture.

"It is good to see you again," Aurra's cat-like eyes narrowed and shifted to Luke. "What do you have for us this time?' He asked glancing back to Zabi.

"Something for your boss," Zabi answered, "Take us to him."

"As you wish," Aurra bowed slightly in respect to his guest, then led Zabi to a nearby building that towered above their heads like a huge granite monolith. The sun reflected from its surface making it gleam in the bright afternoon light.

They entered and took the lift to the fifteenth floor where Aurra led them to a waiting area outside Dengar's office, "Have a seat," he stepped to a desk against the opposite wall and called Dengar. He listened for a moment.

Zabi lowered himself into a chair and considered how to present his information. He needed to be sure he framed Bove as a real threat and decided their encounter with him would show him in the light he wanted to portray. *That should be enough to convince them*, he leaned back in his chair stretching his legs out.

"Dengar will see you now," Aurra stepped to the door resting a paw on the handle. Zabi and Luke entered Dengar's office. Dengar stood up behind his desk, he wore attire similar to Arrua, but in green that set off his deep brown fur. Strips of lighter brown shot through his facial fur and down his neck looking like the strips covered his entire body. He wasn't as bulky as Aurra, yet his build was solid. He smiled showing sharp teeth lining his jaws, "Zabi," he said clasping his paw over his chest and nodding to Luke. He sat extending his arm towards the chairs facing the desk, "What do you have for us this time? More weapons, I hope."

"Well, yes, I do have some hand cannons especially made for your soldiers."

"How many?" Dengar asked, impatient as usual. The Kazons were notorious for their lack of small talk. And Dengar wasted no time with idle chatter.

"Two hundred," Zabi said. He thought he should ask for Varian Renneski--Deputy of the military–to join them, but then he figured Dengar was the better choice for his information about Bove. "But," he continued, "I'm not here to sell weapons. I have news concerning your planet, Kryth."

"Does this have to do with Earth's colonists? We have informed Earth of their violation and are waiting to hear from them. So, what news do you have?'

"Well," Zabi considered how to say it, "I have information that Earth has a spy on his way to learn about Kryth."

"What does he want?"

"Well, I don't know exactly, probably anything to do with your military, and the situation on Kryth. Whatever he wants, he can't be trusted. I would not let him land if it were up to me."

"How do you know this?"

"I have had dealings with him before. Not long ago he stole a shipment of weapons from me. He cost me a hundred thousand credits." Zabi watched Dengar as he considered the information. He added, "Anything he can learn he will take back to Earth. Be very careful, he's tricky and you can't trust him."

"How do you know he's coming here?" Dengar asked again, anger lacing his voice. His eyes fixed on Zabi waiting for an answer.

"I have good sources," Zabi smiled hoping to ease Dengar's concerns.

"Good sources? Are they reliable, trustworthy?"

"Absolutely." Zabi knew he was taking a risk, if Tom were lying to him, which he doubted, he could be in serious trouble. The Kazons don't take well to lies and if caught in one it could mean his life. Zabi held his breath hoping Dengar would accept his story.

"When will this spy be arriving?" Dengar asked studying Zabi closely, watching for a tick of an eye, or a bead of sweat to betray him. He saw none.

"In the next few days, maybe a week or two."

"A week or two? Or a couple of days? Which is it?"

"Within two weeks," Zabi said and hoped he was right. He will be in deep trouble if Bove takes longer or doesn't arrive at all. He knew he was taking a chance, but he believed Tom had been truthful in trying to save himself.

"You will remain here until your spy arrives. We will need you to identify him."

"Of course," Zabi agreed.

"Now," Dengar said, "what do you want for the hand cannons?"

"Ah, the hand cannons," Zabi felt a surge of relief ripple through his body. "They cost me fifty-eight thousand credits, so to cover the purchase and delivery costs I can't take less than ninety thousand."

"We'll give you seventy-five."

"Eighty," Zabi countered.

"Seventy-five," Dengar repeated, then to Aurra. "See that they're unloaded at once. And let Varian know of their receipt. Get all the information about Zabi's spy before he leaves." He gave Zabi a look of warning and stood indicating the meeting was done.

Aurra nodded to him and then ushered Zabi out to the waiting area. He questioned him about Bove and recorded everything Zabi told him. When finished he said, "Your credits will be deposited in your account once the goods are verified and accepted."

"Very good," Zabi said. "When will you be picking up the cannons?"

"That's not my decision, Dengar will let you know. Now, if you will excuse me," Aurra said showing Zabi and Luke the exit.

When they entered the lift, Zavi said, "We need to find a way off this rock. I don't want to be here when Bove arrives, he may have documentation justifying his request and that will cause a lot of trouble for us."

"I agree," Luke said, "But how will we get away?"

"Let me think on that." Zabi pressed the pad for the first floor.

# Eighteen

"The cesium mines are in the mountains to the east of the city," Zohn explained as he escorted them to a transport. "We'll take this part way, but there's no place to land at the mines," he smiled at Stella touching her elbow to help her in. "A tractor lift will take us the rest of the way," he followed her in ignoring Bove.

Bove clenched his fists, then spread his fingers wide as he reached for the handle at the transport door. He pulled himself in only to find Zohn sitting next the Stella speaking softly. He flopped down across from them and intentionally looked away, then back at them. He wanted to interrupt, but he knew if he spoke, he might ruin this whole trip. So, he sat in frustration watching Zohn make advances to Stella.

After a short flight, the transport lowered onto a landing pad, Zohn ushered Stella out followed by Bove, "Wait here while I get us a tractor lift," he said and headed for a small building close by.

"He seems taken with you," Bove said to Stella trying not to sound jealous, then wishing he had kept his mouth shut.

"Nonsense," she snapped, "he's only trying to be friendly, and we need him on our side. Remember your place."

"Yeah," Bove said as he saw Zohn exit the building in a tractor lift.

Once in the lift, they were off running along a narrow road leading to the mines. They made their way winding through a thick forest of pine trees covering the mountain like a heavy blanket. The air was dense and filled with the scent of the forest duff and pine needles. An easy breeze swept the aroma through the trees and into the tractor lift's cabin. Bove inhaled the smell while Stella waved it away.

"How much farther?" She asked.

We're close. The mines are just over the next rise," Zohn sounded like he was hiding something, making both Stella and Bove uneasy. But as they crested the hill the mines came into view. Covering the valley below were small shed-like buildings in front of each mine entrance. A total of six mines lined the valley walls with tracks running from each mine entrance to a nearby shed. Coming out of each shed, the tracks continued to a central structure, and leaving from there was a single track that came up from the valley alongside the road where the tractor lift sat. A cart came out of one mine loaded with raw ore and disappeared into the shed close to the entrance.

"The ore," Zohn said as he started down the slope toward the mines, "is sifted for raw cesium in the sorting buildings and then sent to the main loading station to be packaged for shipment to a refinery. We process twenty-two thousand kilos a week from all six mines. More than enough to supply your four thousand, don't you think?" Zohn gave Stella a sweet smile, then turned to Bove, "And you, Bove, what do you think?" He stopped in front of one of the sheds.

Stella gave Bove a stare and a slight shake of her head, Bove shrugged. "Quite impressive," he said.

Zohn stared for a moment, wheels turning in his head, "Your accent. Are you from Earth?"

"Yes," Stella cut in. "He's immigrated recently and has applied for citizenship. He will be a Ceti-2 citizen within a month."

"Is that right?" Zohn studied Stella closely all business. "We've done some research, and it seems Bove has not immigrated anywhere. In fact, he is still an Earth citizen."

Stella's eyes narrowed and darkened, "You checked us out?" Her voice rose a pitch.

"Wait," Bove interceded, but before he could continue Stella cut him off.

"Take us back. If you can't trust us, we won't be doing any trading. We can leave when you get us back to our shuttle."

"Don't be rash," Zohn said, "Nothing has been decided. We only checked your story for our own safety. The same thing you would have done under the same circumstances. Is that not true?"

Stella stared at him, then slowly nodded her head.

"I can explain," Bove said.

"When we return to the capital, we will discuss everything. Now let us enjoy our excursion and see the mines."

*   *   *

Firaaz was sitting in the conference room holding a data pad when they returned from the mine excursion. Bove and Stella sat opposite him and waited. Zohn entered and took a seat glancing at Stella with a slight smile. Firaaz said, "Well, the committee has made a decision not to trade with you," he looked directly at Stella.

"For what reason?" Anger clouded her face.

"It's not due to you," Firaaz assured her with a tight smile, "but Bove. The committee refuses to deal with an Earthling." Firaaz glanced at Bove and quickly back to Stella, "With that said, I hope you enjoyed your tour of the mines. I always find them quite interesting." He intentionally avoided looking at Bove.

Sidestepping the change of subject, Stella said, "You're not dealing with him, you're dealing with me, and I'm not from Earth. My pilot has nothing to do with this deal."

"It doesn't matter." Firaaz glanced at Zohn and then smiled at Stella.

"I would like to speak with the committee," she said. "There are things they should know before making such a decision."

"The decision has been made. There's no need to speak with anyone other than me," Firaaz said.

"This concerns the Kazons," Bove spoke up. "They have claimed ownership of an earth colony and threaten military action if the colonists aren't removed."

"That's Earth's problem. Now, as I said, the decision is made. So, please, let's not dwell on the subject."

"I believe you don't understand," Bove continued. "If this becomes a conflict the Kazons will consider all Earth colonies as enemies. They'll make no distinction." He pushed his point harder, "Sancus will be a fair target for any Kazon warships." He paused to let that statement settle in Firaaz's mind. "Is Sancus prepared to defend against a Kazon attack?"

Firaaz took a breath and stared at Bove. After a moment he said, "I'll speak to the committee." And with no further interaction, he stood and left.

Zohn smiled at Stella, "Well, we'll let Firaaz handle that. Is there anything I might interest you in?

Anything you would like to see while here? We have some interesting museums." His words fell like dry autumn leaves, quietly dying in the silence of the room.

"We'll return to our shuttle," Stella said, "You can reach us there when Firaaz has something to say."

After waiting thirty minutes., they received a communication from Firaaz requesting them to return.

"I have a bad feeling about this," Bove said. "I'm going to warn the crew." He stepped to the front of the shuttle and sent a yellow alert which informed the crew to prepare to leave. "Okay, let's see what they have to say."

# Nineteen

Bove and Stella had been on Sancus for over four hours when they notified the crew of the tour of the cesium mines. They hadn't said how long the tour would take so no one was worried that they hadn't heard from them. Lucy expected their stay to take up most of the day, so having slept little the night before, she took the time in her cabin for a rest.

She couldn't help but wonder what was happening on Sancus, were they making a deal, still touring the mines, or were there problems? Had the Sancusians discovered Bove was from Earth and done something to him? She pushed those thoughts from her mind and focused.

She was good at that, having graduated at the top of her class from a prestigious university—The Capital Institute of Future Science. She had a double major in Cyber Security and Advanced Astro Physics making her the ideal candidate to operate the computer systems on a starship.

After graduation, she joined the military as a computer expert but being a woman in a man's world she found her assignments were less than challenging leaving her bored and unfulfilled. When her three-year commitment was completed, she left the military and looked for something more exciting—more challenging. But found herself on the Ibex taking orders from Lucus and wishing she had stayed in the military, but hindsight is all-seeing. Since Bove had taken over the Ibex things had become more interesting. She found herself taking a stand when Bove had defied Lucus, and she had risen to confront Zabi with the rest of the crew. All the while backing Bove to rescue Stella. It made her realize she was stronger than she thought and didn't have to be afraid. She was done being pushed around like a junior member of the crew. Now they were on another mission that could be dangerous, and challenging. She was glad to have Bove as the captain. Not only did he bring excitement, but he was fair and considerate of the crew in any decisions. And he had trusted her with a secret—his visions.

She had become captivated after hearing about his experience. Two things about them had been disturbing her and she needed new ideas. His broken bones had healed in a single day and that was not possible. Bones take at least six weeks to completely heal. Bove saw the scans the doctor ran, and even the doctor couldn't believe what he was seeing. He planned to do more research, but he never had the chance to follow up.

Lucy, with her understanding of astrophysics, was able to think outside the conventional frame of reference and delve into abstract ideas like space-time manipulation. Considering the two facts Bove had told her, she concluded that first more than a single day had passed during his vision, and second, he could not have been in two places at the same time.

He told her the vision occurred while he was in sickbay where someone would have checked on him at some point during the night. So, if he was on the planet of three hills, they would have missed him. That was not the case, as he had told her, when he woke everyone acted as if he slept through the night. So, if no one noticed him missing how could he be in a different location for a full day? This could be explained if Bove was in a dream state.

In a dream, one could experience a much longer time than the dream takes. She had dreams that spanned several days, and some dreams that felt real. A dreamer could think they were living the experience. So, Bove's visions could have been from being in a dream state where time accelerated making him believe he was experiencing hours or days passing when only minutes had elapsed. In Bove's vision, he could have been induced into a dream state to live the time in the vision.

Concluding that, Lucy decided the vision was an experience of compressed time projected into Bove's mind, so he thought he was actually on a different planet for a complete day when in fact he was simply having a realistic dream, or vision as he described it. That was a good theory but how could something like that be done? He was in sick bay, so doctors and nurses had access to him, as well as almost anyone on the ship. But why would anyone, doctors, nurses, or anyone else, want to induce a dream state with no outcome but to force Bove to help people?

Lucy could not think of a way to force a dream state and if it were possible, how would someone induce a specific dream? *No! It's not possible.* So, she had no explanation of how he experienced a whole day while in sick bay under the watch of a night nurse.

The other thing about his vision was the healing of his arm and foot. Even if the bones were not broken and they were only bruised, it would not clear up in a single day. Bove said the scans were showing the bones completely healed. No sign of a fracture or break. Considering those facts meant he had to be gone for at least six weeks. *How is that possible?* She wondered.

Shifting her thinking to the abstract she considered first the location change. If Bove was really on a different planet, or at least off the ship, how could that be done? Simply by abducting him and taking him elsewhere. Intruders could have evaded any alarm in the ship and knocked him out then taken him off the ship. Once off the ship, they could place him on the planet of three hills.

*That's a good possibility, but he would have been missing if a nurse checked on him, but he wasn't.* Getting more abstract, she considered another possibility, time manipulation. If the vision creators were able to manipulate time so the ship experienced only seconds while Bove experienced days that would explain why he wasn't missed during the night. Then it dawned on her that both issues could be explained under that scenario. Slow down or stop time long enough for Bove to heal and experience the day on the hills.

*But how would something like that be done?* There would have to be a device to control time in a certain location while it moved along in another location.

Lucy dropped her head into her hands and rubbed her eyes. That certainly explained the vision, but it would take more time to learn how it was controlled.

She cleared her head of these thoughts, crawled into her bed, and was asleep as her blanket covered her.

*     *     *

The incessant beep of the communicator woke her with a start. She fumbled at her night table for the button to answer the alarm, "What!" She almost shouted, still half asleep.

"We need you on the bridge." It was Jack, calm and controlled, just telling the facts. "We might have an issue down below. Bove sent a stand-by warning."

It took a minute for that to sink into her still half-asleep mind. As the information sank in, she responded, "A warning? What kind of warning?"

"Just get up here," Jack said calmly.

She rolled out of her bunk, threw her clothes on, pushed her hair back into a ponytail, splashed water on her face, and headed out.

She made it to the bridge in three minutes and slid into her chair. She tapped a couple of pads to activate her display and started scanning the output. She was looking at the ship's status as well as any data from the surface. "The shuttle is clear," she touched more pads on her keyboard, "but Bove or Stella aren't in it. Scanning to find them." She concentrated on her console.

"What did the message say?" Dan had been called from sleep as was evident from his bedhead. He sipped a cup of coffee.

"Nothing, just stand by. No details. It was a yellow alert." Jack told him.

"Maybe it's nothing," Lucy said. "Maybe they just want us to prepare to leave quickly."

"Yeah, maybe," Jack agreed.

"They're in the complex," Lucy added. "That must be where they're meeting."

"Any other messages?" Ryan asked.

"Nope," Jack answered. "There must be something going on or Bove wouldn't send a yellow alert. There's no need to leave quickly if things are okay. I'll set a transit location just in case. Lucy be ready to transit if we need to. Dan keep weapons ready but don't arm them yet. We don't want to antagonize them."

"Roger that," Dan said tapping the pads in front of him. "Weapons ready for arming," he confirmed.

*What's going on?* Lucy wondered. She knew Bove was cautious in dangerous situations, but this was supposed to be a simple trade agreement. That is if Bove stayed quiet.

# Twenty

Zohn greeted Bove and Stella at the shuttle door, he was alone and guided them to the transport sitting on the next pad. They climbed in and were off to the government complex.

Once there, they entered the conference room and as they started to take their seats two soldiers came in and another stayed outside next to the door. Firaaz stood and waved a hand for Bove and Stella to sit. A soldier hovered near each of them. Bove felt a shiver run across his shoulders and down his spine.

Stella, still standing, glanced at Bove, "What's the meaning of this?" She stepped away from the soldier.

Firaaz held up a hand, "Please," he waved a hand at the soldier to step away. "This is not what you think," he said looking at Stella with a slight smile, "Please sit."

"Then what is it?" Bove asked and stepped toward the door, but the soldier blocked him. Muscles tightened in his arms. He considered his options.

"Please," Firaaz said again reaching a hand toward the chairs.

"Tell us what's going on," Bove glanced over his shoulder at the soldier.

"As promised, I met with the council, and they have decided to keep Bove here." He added quickly, "Stella you are free to go."

"What?" Bove's voice rose as he glared at Firaaz.

"Only until we confirm your story," Firaaz stated.

"That's unacceptable," Stella said rounding on the soldier ready to defend herself. Bove did the same only to step into a stunner. He stumbled and sank into a chair. The soldier grabbed Stella by both arms clamping them to her sides. Struggling did no good as the grip tightened.

"Like I said," Firaaz checked Bove and turned to Stella, "you are free to go. We'll let you know our decision."

The soldier turned Stella to the door and forced her through, down the hall, and into the transport despite her fighting and complaining.

*        *        *

Bove, still weak from the stun, was sitting where he had collapsed. The door to the room was closed and a soldier posted outside. He quickly began to recover from the stun wondering what had happened. His whole body ached down to his bones and his thoughts were fuzzy. He slumped in the chair waiting for his head to clear and his bones to stop aching. Slowly he pushed himself up and looked around.

The room was empty, chairs pushed in toward the table, blinds covering the windows, and a guard visible through the glass. He was alone, "Hey!" he yelled. The guard glanced around then turned back facing away from him. He stood hoping his legs would hold him and stumbled to the door only to find it locked and the guard unresponsive.

*What now*, he shoved his hands in his pockets to find them empty. He tapped his ear to find his communicator gone, no way to communicate, no tools to free himself, nothing. He tried the door again, still locked. The window blinds opened easily letting sunlight in and giving him a view from the fifteenth floor. *No escaping through that*, he sank back into the chair easing the pain in his bones, and waited.

*        *        *

The transport dropped Stella and a guard at her shuttle and before leaving, the driver told her to return to her ship. The guard made sure she understood that she should leave and stepped to the edge of the landing pad.

*Damn!* She turned toward the guard who nodded for her to enter the shuttle. *The nerve of them! They have no right keeping him like he's a criminal!* She kicked the step leading into the shuttle then entered and took the pilot's seat. "Ibex," she said, "Stella here. I'll be returning shortly, and I'll explain everything when I get there. *They'll let me know their decision.* "Shit!" she shouted into the cabin.

"Acknowledged," Jack said.

She fired the engines and headed for the Ibex. It took five minutes to reach orbit and settle into the shuttle bay.

When she reached the bridge, the crew was there, waiting. She explained the situation.

"What do you mean they're holding him?" Jack demanded.

"Listen," Stella said. "There's nothing we can do right now. There's an army out there we can't fight. We tried talking to them and this is the result."

"We need to rescue him," Dan said. "There must be a way to get to him, to free him."

Stella shook her head, "That's a bad idea. We need to wait this out. If they contact Ceti-2 they'll verify our story."

"And if they contact Earth, will they back our story?" Jack asked.

"I think they already have, and Earth didn't back us. But they wouldn't know of Bove's decision to defect to Ceti-2." Stella crossed her arms over her chest. "But intervening will destroy any chance of getting the cesium, and probably leave Bove in prison. All we can do is wait."

"Actually, there's plenty we can do," Lucy said turning to her console and starting to type.

"What do you mean?" Ryan asked.

"Watch," Lucy continued to type, "I can locate his bio signs with our new sensors." She flipped her wrist and a map appeared on the main view screen at the front of the bridge. "There," she said pointing to the screen where a blue dot pulsed. "He's there. All we have to do is go down and get him."

"No, we're not going anywhere," Stella glared at Lucy. "It's good to know where he is though."

"It's not your decision, Sella," Jack said, "Bove left me in charge, and I'll decide our next move," his voice rose with tension.

"And what would that be?" Stella snapped back.

"Well, for now," he paused, looked at Lucy, then shrugged his shoulders, "we'll wait since we know where he is. Can you tell what condition he's in?"

"He looks fine, all his vitals are good."

"And where is that?" Jack asked pointing to the blue dot.

Before Lucy could answer, Stella leaned over her shoulder, "That's where we met. They haven't moved him, probably just locked him in the room."

"Okay," Jack said. "If this goes on very long, we're doing something."

"Understood," Stella agreed. "Let me know if you hear anything," she stood and headed out.

Lucy watched her leave. *This isn't right*, she pushed her chair back and followed her out to the lift. "Hold it," she said hurrying in.

The lift door closed when Stella pressed the pad for deck four. Lucy turned to her, "You don't seem too concerned about this," she said.

"What do you know about how I feel?" Stella retorted.

"I can only go by your reactions," Lucy pressed against the lift wall. "You came back seemingly unconcerned that Bove's left behind, and say we just wait. Aren't you concerned about him? Or do you only care about the cesium?"

"Of course I'm concerned about him," she glared at Lucy, anger and worry reflected on her face. "But there's the ship and you—the crew—to think about. If we do anything there's the Sancusian military waiting to stop us. And if you have forgotten, I'm familiar with the Sancusians. I've dealt with them before. They may be quick to hold someone, but they'll listen to reason and once they speak with my government, they'll let him go. It's only a matter of time."

Stella stepped out of the lift when the door opened on deck four. Lucy followed quietly. She wasn't sure what to make of Stella's comments. Yet she seemed genuinely concerned about Bove from her reaction to her comment about the cesium. She followed her into the kitchen.

Stella turned, "Are you following me?" She asked.

"What? No." Lucy stepped back, hesitated, and ran her hands down the front of her top smoothing it. "No," she repeated. "I'm going to get something to eat."

Stella looked at her then turned and headed to the back where the real kitchen was, "Well what are you thinking of having?" She asked.

"I don't know. Whatever's easy."

"You cook?"

"Yeah, some."

Stella rummaged through the cupboard and put a variety of items on the counter. She found meat in the refrigerator and added it to the collection. "Let's see what we can come up with," she opened a box of pasta and began putting ingredients into a pot.

They worked together making their meal then sat across from each other with plates of food.

"What do you think?" Stella asked.

"Good," Lucy took a bite. "So, you do care what happens to Bove,' she studied Stella.

Stella looked up from her food, a frown creasing her brow, "Of course I do."

"I mean more than the captain," Lucy watched for Stella's reaction and saw a flicker of realization on her face.

"Yeah," she said hesitantly, "I guess I do." She glanced at Lucy, then looked away dropping her fork on the plate. "That's very observant of you, but the rest of the crew doesn't need to know."

"Oh, of course not."

"And you? What are your feelings?"

"He's the captain, that's all." That wasn't entirely true since he had trusted her with his visions, but she wasn't going to tell Stella that. "Are you going to stay after we get the cesium?"

"We'll see," Stella picked up her fork and took a bite. "It depends. If Bove wants me around or not."

"You would be helpful dealing with the Kazons."

"Yeah, I suppose so."

"Have you dealt with them before?"

"Some, they're not easy," Stella looked up at the ceiling. "But they do need cesium, so we should be able to trade with them."

"Yeah," Lucy said. "So, you've dealt with them before?"

Stella pushed her chair from the table. "We had a revolution recently and I made a deal with them for some weapons—the ones you helped me with. They were very suspicious of my motives, but I was able to convince them I only wanted to stop the revolution. They finally believed me and sold me the weapons."

"That must have been hard," Lucy pushed her empty plate away.

"Yeah. So, what about you, what's your story?"

Lucy hesitated for a second, "Not much to tell." She wondered why Stella asked about her, was it interest in her? "Well," she continued, "I spent three years in the service, then got a job on the Ibex." She stopped and looked at Stella who remained quiet waiting for more. "That's pretty much it," she finished.

"I'm sure there's more," Stella said, "You'll have to fill me in later."

"And you, what's your story?" Lucy asked.

"Like yours, mine will have to wait until later."

Lucy nodded in understanding.

# Twenty-One

Tom looked through the force field at a hallway filled with dim light. Stale air irritated his nose and sweat beaded on his forehead. He wiped his brow to ease his nerves while he listened for any sounds. The announcement about the two days of shore leave was heard throughout the ship, so he was betting on that for his freedom. After waiting thirty minutes he hoped everyone was off the ship and having a good time ashore.

*It's a good thing they didn't search me thoroughly,* he reached into a hidden pocket in his jacket to retrieve the magnetic key he carried to open the cargo pens. The lock was next to the door on the opposite side of the wall, but the key was powerful enough to trigger it. He smiled when the force field vanished, and he stepped through the doorway. The way to the airlock was clear in his mind and a quick exit would lessen the chance of being caught. When he reached the airlock, it was closed, as expected, but opened easily to allow a view out onto the spaceport. There was activity around some of the other ships, but no sign of the crew or Zabi. *Good,* he stepped off the ship.

He was free but on an unfamiliar planet with no idea where to go to find help. A ship nearby had activity around the cargo ramp and as he approached a worker turned towards him. The cat-like features startled him for a moment, but he quickly recovered his composure and asked, "Who's ship is this?"

"Who are you? I don't recognize you. Are you new to the crew?" The worker's eyes narrowed, and he showed his teeth—white and sharp.

Tom thought about that question for a moment, then decided the truth was best. "No," he said, "I'm looking for passage off this planet."

"Well, I can't help you." The worker turned back to his task.

"You didn't answer my question, who's ship is it?"

The worker turned back, anger flooding his face. His whiskers twitched and the fur on his face stood out like tiny barbs, "That is none of your business. Now, is it?"

Tom backed off not wanting any trouble, "I'm just looking to get off this planet is all." He turned to leave.

"Check the Radit Inn," the other worker said without turning to look at him.

"Urmph…" said the first worker.

"Uh, thanks?" Tom ventured. He headed for the terminal and the exit into the city.

Without a data pad or Opticom, he didn't know where to start to look for the Radit Inn. But like most cities on Earth and many colonies, there were AutoCabs, and he found one waiting outside the port. He slid into the rear seat and instructed it to take him to the Radit Inn.

"The Radit Inn is three kilometers from here as the map indicates." The cab said. "Please enter payment of fifteen credits." Tom considered his next move, he had credits but on Ardonia, they were inaccessible leaving him broke. He quickly scanned the map to get the route clear in his mind, then stepped out of the AutoCab and headed for the inn on foot.

It was a twenty-minute walk to the three-story building off the main road in a busy part of the city. Its location was convenient to the spaceport and although it wasn't the best accommodation, it was clean and comfortable looking.

The inside was quiet—reserved--and Tom found it comforting. He stepped into the bar and asked for something strong. The bartender looked at him for a moment, "You're new here," it wasn't a question.

Tom nodded, "Yeah, it's my first time."

"Well, we have Toz, a blend of local fermented berries much like Earth's whisky."

"I'll have that," Tom eased onto a bar stool.

"You staying long?" The bartender set a glass of Toz and a bowl of various seeds on the bar in front of Tom.

"Actually, I'm looking for a lift off-planet," Tom answered. Then added, "The ship I arrived on has left without me."

"That's too bad.'

"Yeah, I was delayed and didn't make it back in time. But that was understood, so there're no hard feelings." Tom took a sip of his drink and let the smooth liquid slip down his throat, warming him as it went.

"Well, you might be in luck. There are usually a few pilots that stop in before leaving. So, you might find one with a spare seat." The bartender smiled and moved down the bar to attend to another customer.

Tom had hoped as much. He couldn't spend too much time before finding a way off the planet. Zabi would soon find him gone and start a search, and his crew knew the city much better than him. A glance around the room assured him there were no newcomers. He took another sip and closed his eyes, taking a moment to compose himself.

*       *       *

Their business finished with Dengar, Zabi, and Carter returned to the ship to help with the unloading of the weapons. "They'll be here soon for the hand cannons," Zabi said. "Get the crates out to the holding bay and ready to offload." He headed for his office.

He thought the seventy-five thousand credits would suffice. It was a profit of forty thousand, *not bad*. They would celebrate once they're allowed to leave, and Luke can take care of Tom, *He'll come up with a suitable method*, Zabi assured himself. *He thinks the airlock is too quick, and maybe he's right*, he mused. Tom had to go just to ensure he didn't warn Bove of the setup. Zabi smiled to himself, *and Bove, he'll rot in a Kazon prison. Maybe I'll go after his ship If I remember right that little brunette would be a nice addition to my crew, yeah, she'd do nicely...*

Two hours later Carter strolled into Zabi's office, "everything in the holding bay is ready to be unloaded." He said taking a seat.

"Very good."

"When will they be here for it?"

"They didn't say," Zabi answered. "Wait for them down there."

"Yes, sir," Carter said and left.

After another hour Carter contacted Zabi to tell him they had arrived.

"Give them any help they need," Zabi told him, then wondered where Luke was. He wanted to settle how to get rid of Tom, but then he wondered if he should hold onto him until Bove turned up. That would be best if Tom was trying to buy time, it wouldn't work. *He's got to go!* He contacted Carter again, "Get the crew back. As soon as the cannons are unloaded, we're leaving."

"Will do, captain," Carter answered.

An hour later Luke strolled into Zabi's office, "We're leaving?"

"Yeah, as soon as those cannons are unloaded and hauled off."

Zabi leaned back in his chair studying Luke. "Have you decided what to do with Tom?"

"Oh, yeah. When can I start?"

"As soon as we're out of this system," Zabu smiled.

Luke smiled back and stood to leave.

Five minutes later Luke contacted Zabi," Where's Tom?" His voice trembled with anger.

"In the brig," Zabi said.

"No, he's not!" Luke was furious and unable to keep it from showing in his voice. "He's gone!"

"What?" Zabi paused for a second. "Search the ship. Is the rest of the crew back? If not get them here. We need to find that son-of-a-bitch!" He slammed his fist on the desk. "Damn it!" He swore they would search the ship, then the spaceport, then the town. The whole damn planet if they had to. He would not get away. He's probably already warned Bove. *Oh, when I get my hands on him!*

*     *     *

The bartender alerted Tom and nodded toward the man who walked in. Tom watched as he took a seat at a nearby table and ordered a drink. He wasn't sure if he was someone that could give him a ride, or not, but either way, he had to find transport. He stepped to the table, "Hi," he said looking down at a man with dark hair, a firm mouth, and suspicious eyes.

He looked up scanning Tom from head to boots, "I'm not looking for company," he said.

"Maybe not," Tom said, "but could you use a weapons handler?"

"You're looking for a job?" The man looked closer at him, "What's your skills?"

"Weapons and cargo," Tom said taking a seat across from him. He knew weapons experts were in short supply and having someone that could work them was a plus for any ship.

"How did you end up out of work here? Most crews stay close to their ship in case they need to leave quickly. After all, this is Ardonia and they're not real friendly to us."

"It's a long story. A misunderstanding and I was left by mistake."

"Won't they be back for you?"

"Not soon. So, can you use another crew member?"

'I'll give you a ride to my next stop. If you prove valuable, we'll see. That work for you?"

"Yeah," Tom felt his shoulder relax and a smile trying to express itself. "When do you leave?"

"Tomorrow, sunrise. Be at pad 18D."

Tom looked at him for a moment, cleared his throat, and said, "Since I'm stranded with no credits could I spend the night on board?"

"Absolutely not. I don't know you or what your game is. I've offered you a ride so don't push it." He stared at Tom with hard eyes and a firm mouth, "Understood?"

Tom nodded, "Yeah, understood." He paused and started to stand, "What should I call you?"

"Captain will do. Don't be late, I won't wait for you." He turned back to his drink dismissing Tom.

Tom went back to his bar stool happy with the offer, but he wondered where he was going to spend the night. With no credits available he needed someplace Zabi wouldn't look for him, but where? An idea formed. He waved the bartender over and told him Captain would pay the tab, then he left quickly.

Outside he looked around watching for any sign of Zabi and his crew, all was quiet. Searching the area for a secluded spot where he could hide, he came to a park thick with bushes. Feeling this would work he settled down for what he hoped would be an uneventful night. He was wrong.

Darkness had settled over the park like a thick cloud covering everything. Tom had settled into a light sleep only to be awakened by a prod in his side. He was on his feet in an instant ready to defend himself when another poke hit him in the gut. He lashed out with a fist at the only target he saw and at the last instance, he realized the person standing in front of him was a Kazon security guard.

The guard stood four inches shorter than Tom and was in a crisp clean uniform. The fur on his face glistened in the moonlight and his whiskers twitched. Tom tried to pull his punch but was too late. His fist connected with the guard's jaw hard enough to knock him back a couple of steps. As Tom was trying to pull his arm back another prod poked his side. This one was activated. He felt the shock flare from his side up and down his body followed by numbness through his arms and legs causing him to fall to the ground. He moaned as his muscles spasmed shaking him like leaves in a breeze. Then darkness overtook him.

*    *    *

Zabi searched the entire Dark Star then had the crew move to the spaceport and then out to the town. Darkness covered the spaceport when the crew stepped from the ship making the search slow and filled with uncertainty. Three hours passed with no success. The taverns, hotels, cafes, and any place they thought Tom would hold up were searched with no luck. The only lead they got was at the Radit Inn where the bartender confirmed Tom was there, but he had no idea where Tom had gone to. Finally, after midnight they agreed that they were not going to find him.

"You looked everywhere?" Zabi's face was tight with anger, his fingers curled into fists, his eyes narrowed to slits, and his mouth was a hard line. He turned toward the main screen covering the forward side of the bridge and showing the landing pads surrounding the Dark Star. "How the hell did he get out?" he demanded.

"I don't know!" Luke wanted to scream. He wanted to get rid of Tom more than anyone else on the ship. He was the one that had been shot and his arm still isn't back to normal if it ever would be. So, yeah, he wanted to take care of Tom himself and was furious that he was missing.

"Could he be on one of those ships?" Ruby asked pointing toward the main screen.

"No," Carter said, "we checked them all. The only way he would be on one is if the ship's crew lied to us."

"Maybe you should check them again," Zabi's voice was deadly serious.

"We can't just walk on, and they won't let us on. We asked." Carter said.

"Have any left?" Ruby asked.

"No. They won't leave til morning." Carter answered her.

"Then he's still here," she said.

"Yeah, so?" Luke glared at her. "I say we search again tomorrow. We'll hit the ships first and make sure he's not on one."

"You had better be up early if you want to check all the ships," Carter told him.

'I know which ones to check," Luke said. "We'll get that little shit! He's not getting off this planet. Not if I can help it."

"I'll give it three days," Zabi said. "After that, we leave with or without Tom. Is that clear?"

The crew nodded, although Luke and Carter grumbled disagreements. Then Luke said, "Would it hurt to stay a day or two longer?"

"We'll leave in three days. I don't want to be around in case Bove never shows up. So, yes it would hurt." Zabi glared at Luke with a look that shot fear through him. He looked away.

Their search resumed the next morning with no better luck. Zabi contacted the Kazon security command and asked if Bove had arrived. He had not. This continued for three days with no sign that Tom was still on Kazon. Zabi became more frustrated as each day slipped by. Tom had vanished, there was no sign of Bove, and the crew was becoming increasingly agitated. Zabi decided they would leave the next morning whether they found Tom or not. Bove would show up or not, either way, the Kazons be damn. He was sure they wouldn't try to stop him, that could be considered an act of war. So, his mind was made up.

# Twenty-Two

MingBourne was the original base founded on Sancus and as it grew, more bases were set up and they grew into cities spawning small towns relying on them for support and protection. These became five districts, each wanting independence and a say in the decisions affecting the planet, and so the council was born made up of a representative from each district.

Firaaz sat before the council and explained the situation with the Kazons saying in conclusion, "The earthling may be correct in saying the Kazons will look at any earth colony as an enemy putting us in a dangerous position, and we may need the protection from Earth."

All five members of the council objected at once saying they should never accept help from Earth. They claimed they couldn't be trusted.

"They'll renege on any promise and leave us vulnerable to attack?" Valen Kador, the member from Tiporia, said.

"Only if there's war, and there's no sign of that now. We have done quite well without Earth, and this is no reason to depend on them now." Taran Vanlaere, the member from Bildon Point, said.

Nevyn Wakeman, the member from Neo Bidenham, asked, "What did the earthling say about this Kazon threat?"

"Why don't we ask him?" Valen suggested,

"Bring him here," Bedwyr ordered.

Firaaz moved to the far side of the chamber out of sight.

A guard left and returned a couple of minutes later with Bove, he showed him a seat below the dais where the council sat. Bove sank onto the bench and looked up at the council not knowing why he was there.

Bedwyr stared down at him with placid eyes, "What do you know about the Kazons?"

"Not much," Bove said, "They have claimed that Kryth belongs to them, and they want our colonists removed."

"So, what does that have to do with us?" Nevyn asked. "And why does that mean we should trade with you?"

"I have been given the job of finding more information about the Kazons." Bove said, "I'm supposed to find out what they intend to do about the colonists. What their military capabilities are, and if they intend to use them. I can't find that out if I have nothing to trade with them."

"What does trading have to do with gathering information?" Valen asked.

"It's my way to get close to them." Bove checked the council members to figure out their reactions—favorable or not. He could tell nothing.

"And," Taran asked, "why do we have to open a trade agreement with Earth to do that?"

"It doesn't have to be a trade agreement," Bove said, "it can be a one-time trade. Some medical equipment for some cesium. And it's not with Earth, it's with Stella."

The members huddled together and mumbled for a few minutes. Then Bedwyr raised a hand to the guard then pointed to Bove. "Take him back to the conference room." The guard stepped to Bove and escorted him out.

"So," Bedwyr asked, "will we trade the cesium?"

"A better question would be, 'Do we contact Earth?'" Nevyn said.

"Why?" Valen asked. "If we trade the cesium there's no need to call Earth."

Taran raised a hand, "I don't think we should have any contact with Earth."

After a couple of minutes, the other members nodded their heads.

"Agreed, we don't contact Earth?" Bedwyr asked.

The council nodded in agreement.

"So, we'll make the trade," Bedwyr concluded.

*　　　　*　　　　*

It had been four hours since Stella returned from the surface and the tension on the bridge was high. Everyone jumped when the communicator chimed with an incoming message. Stella, sitting on the captain's chair, tapped the communication button and answered, 'Stella Thorne, captain of the Ibex."

"Stella," Firaaz's voice was calm, yet Stella could pick up a slight uncertainty in it.

"Are you going to release Bove?" she asked not letting Firaaz continue.

"Uh," He stammered, "we will."

"When?" She pushed.

"We are in the process as we speak," his voice gained more confidence. "Would you like to return to Mingbourne?"

"This had better not be a trick," Stella warned, "We are not defenseless."

"Please don't do anything rash," Firaaz implored. "This is not a trick. Bove will be waiting for you when you arrive."

Stella switched off the communication and turned to the crew, "Be ready for anything, I don't trust these guys."

"Will do," Jack said nodding to the crew. "Keep me informed," he added to Stella.

She nodded, "Of course."

*       *       *

The shuttle settled on the landing pad and Stella stepped onto the transport waiting there for her. It raced to the Ming Center, and she was ushered into the conference room where Bove sat waiting for her.

"Are you okay?" she asked, concern ringing in her words.

He nodded, "It seemed they have agreed to make a trade." Bove looked at Firaaz sitting at the head of the table, Zohn to his right.

"Is that true?" Stella pulled out a chair and lowered herself into it.

"We have decided to trade some cesium for your medical equipment," Firaaz stated unequivocally. "A shipment of cesium is being readied as we speak."

"When will it be ready, and where should we pick it up?" Stella asked.

"It'll be ready tomorrow morning. We'll send landing coordinates where we'll make the exchange."

"The morning..." Bove started but Stella glanced at him with a slight shake of her head.

"We'll return to our ship and wait for your instructions," she said.

"Very good," Firaaz smiled, "we'll speak in the morning. We'll have your two thousand kilos ready for you."

"Four thousand," Stella emphasized.

"Four thousand, that's right," Firaaz nodded his head.

Stella and Bove boarded their shuttle and closed the door. "Do you believe that?" she asked. "He tried to short us two thousand."

"Doesn't matter, we'll make sure there's four thousand in the morning." Bove started the engines, "They won't get anything until we've verified the amount of cesium. If they short us, we'll hold back the equipment."

*       *       *

Landing instructions were communicated early the next morning. Bove displayed a map of the planet on the main viewing screen and pinpointed the site. "That must be their processing plant," he said.

"Yeah," Stella agreed.

He switched to internal coms and ordered the crew to the conference room. When everyone had arrived, he said, "We've received landing instructions to load the cesium. We'll be taking the Ibex down to transfer the medical equipment for our cesium." He paused, "After what they did before, I don't trust them, so be ready for anything."

"What time will we get it?" Jack asked.

"Four, planet time."

"That gives us nine hours," Lucy said.

"What do we do until then?" Dan asked.

"Move the equipment to the holding area then clear an area in hold A for the cesium. I want the transfer to go as quickly as possible."

"That'll shift the ship's load off balance." Dan had a worried look on his face. "We'll have trouble lifting off."

"One of the things I had B-Rich do was add conduits to shift ballast while in flight, so we won't have any problems."

"Cool," Dan wiped his brow and smiled.

"Let's get to work," Bove slid his seat back and stood up.

By three in the afternoon, they had the equipment ready to unload and an area cleared for the cesium. Bove set the countdown for entry to the atmosphere and the crew ran their checks to verify the ship was ready. After moving the cargo, they had to be sure everything was secure. If cargo started to move around in the bays it could cause the ship to crash. That's the last thing they needed.

The checks came back good, they had the green light to break orbit and descend. Ryan set the retro rockets to fire in fifteen minutes to bring them down to the landing site they were given. Fifteen minutes later they fired and the Ibex broke orbit and entered the atmosphere forcing everyone back in their seats. The descent was only three minutes, and when they reached the site, Ryan set the Ibex down precisely where the instructions said.

"Wait here," Bove told the crew, "Prepare to leave. I'll make sure the cesium is correct and then we'll swap the loads. Stella, you're with me. Dan, you, and Lucy prepare to unload the equipment and load the cesium. Decide who will do what." He got up and headed off the bridge followed by Stella. Dan and Lucy were close behind.

Stepping out of the airlock they were met by Firaaz and Zohn, "Greetings," Firaaz said with a slight bow. "We have your cesium ready to load."

"Four thousand kilos?" Stella looked into Firaaz's face looking for deception.

"That's correct," he answered her without a flicker of concern. "You have our equipment?"

"Ready to unload just as soon as we verify the cesium," Bove looked around, "Where is it?"

"I'll have it brought out," Firaaz motioned to a worker who walked off towards a nearby building, and in a few minutes, three tractor loaders came out carrying the cesium and stopped two meters from Bove and Stella. "Where do you load?" Firaaz asked.

Stella walked to the loader farthest away and checked the cesium. Coming back, she stopped at each loader and checked. "Looks good," she told Bove.

Bove tapped his communicator, "Open the cargo doors, we're ready to load." He turned to Firaaz, "The other bay," he pointed to the far side of the ship, "you'll find the equipment. One of the crew is there to help unload."

Firaaz motioned to another worker to head that way. Zohn followed the three tractor lifts as they rolled to cargo bay B.

The entire process took less than two hours, and the cargo was loaded and secured. Bove and Stella said their goodbyes to Firaaz and Zohn.

Back on the bridge, the crew completed preparation for lift-off and Bove gave the order. Ryan fired the engines and the Ibex lifted off Sancus with its load of cesium. "Jack set a course for Ardonia near the system's edge," Bove instructed,

"Yes sir."

"Lucy," he added, "prepare to transit."

"Yes sir," Lucy responded.
"Ryan, get us clear of Sancus."
"Yes sir," Ryan confirmed.
"Once we're clear, transit."

# Twenty-Three

Security was high around Ardonia with six major docking stations ringing the planet, each guarded by three star cruisers. One approached as the Ibex passed the orbit of the outer moon and entered Ardonia space. It was an intimidating craft with laser guns mounted on the top, bottom, front, and back and six big plasma guns lining both sides. Plasma guns of that size fired at once could vaporize a star-destroyer. No telling what a single gun would do to the Ibex. It was considerable firepower and too close for comfort.

"State your business," came through the ship's com port followed by silence.

Bove glanced at the crew, "Here we go," he said and activated the com. "We're a trading vessel here to discuss possible trading arrangements with your government."

"Authorization code," was the response.

"We're new here, asking to discuss trade arrangements. We don't have any codes."

"You and your craft name and designation."

"Bove Sandle, captain of the cargo ship Ibex, a class four freighter."

Silence spread through the bridge as the cruiser hovered near their left side, easily within range to fire on them. Then an order came through the com, "Proceed to docking station D for inspection." The cruiser eased back from the Ibex, turning slowly, then firing its main engine to move farther away. Bove let out the breath he was holding, as did the crew.

"Do it," he ordered Ryan.

The docking station's single bay was empty. Ryan guided the Ibex into it, gently firing the maneuvering thrusters as it closed on the bay. Locking clamps snapped into place on the Ibex's sides and a boarding ramp extended to the airlock on the cargo deck. "Prepare to be boarded for inspection," came an order.

"Acknowledge that," Bove told Jack, then headed for the lift to deck six, "Dan you're with me."

Bove released the airlock and watched the door slide open. Five Kazon security guards with plasma rifles were standing on the boarding ramp. Bove was taken aback by their appearance. They were shorter than Dan and him with broad shoulders and thick arms, fur covered their faces, and ears on the tops of their heads moved independently searching for any sound. One grinned showing pointed teeth and said, "Step aside." Four guards went into the Ibex pushing Bove and Dan aside in the process. Bove started to follow but the last guard stopped him, "Wait outside," he said, then pointing to Dan, "You too." He prodded them by raising and pointing his rifle at Bove, forcing them farther down the ramp. He followed, letting his rifle lower toward the floor, his paw held tight with a finger on the trigger.

"The rest of my crew is still inside," Bove turned toward him.

"You should tell them not to interfere with the inspection," the guard suggested.

Bove clicked his communicator and informed the remaining crew the Kazons had boarded and not to interfere but to watch them. Jack confirmed with a short cryptic *Understood.* After a couple of minutes, another guard approached from inside the station. He nodded in greeting and placed a fist on his chest. He was someone of higher rank and radiated an air of power and self-assurance. Bove copied his greeting with a fist to his chest.

"I am Commander Surton. I oversee this security ring." He straightened his shoulders in a move to show authority. "I have orders to take you into custody."

"What?" Bove felt his gut tighten, as his figures curled into fists.

The guard raised his rifle at Bove. "Back," he said, raising a paw toward Dan. Dan backed up toward the airlock.

Another guard came out of the Ibex with his rifle aiming at Dan "Stand down," he said and stepped past him to Bove.

"What is this about?" Bove asked, raising his hands. "Am I being arrested?"

"Turn around," Surton said. And as Bove turned Surton grabbed his wrist and clamped a restraint on it, then attached it to his other hand.

Two more guards came out circling Bove.

Surton tapped the communicator in his ear, "We have him," he said, then "Yes sir."

He turned to the closest guard, "Bring him," he turned and headed down the ramp. One guard shoved Bove ahead of him and the others followed. Dan watched them go, and the minute they disappeared into the security ring he tapped his communicator, "Jack, we've got a problem." He stepped into the airlock, closed and locked it. "They've taken Bove!"

"What?" The alarm was clear in Jack's voice. "What do you mean, they've taken him?"

"What's going on?" Lucy asked.

"Where are you?" Jack asked Dan.

"I just locked the airlock," Dan said. "They didn't take me."

"You locked it?" Jack almost yelled. "Is the ramp still there?"

"Yeah, I guess."

"What's going on?" Lucy asked again.

"Get up here," Jack said.

"Jack!" Lucy demanded jumping to her feet. "What happened?"

"They've taken Bove," he turned to her.

"They what?" She almost screamed but took a deep breath instead.

"You heard," Jack glanced around, then back to Lucy. "Where's Stella and Ryan?"

"Following the guards, I guess," Lucy answered. "At least they were last I checked."

"Are there any others on board?"

Dan came onto the bridge followed by Ryan. They stopped and looked at everyone. Dan's face was pale, he looked like he would throw up as he fell into Stella's chair.

"Did all the guards leave?" Jack asked. And when Dan didn't respond, he repeated himself louder and pushed Dan's shoulder.

"What?" Dan pulled away and looked up. "What?"

"The guards?" Jack asked again.

"Yeah, they all left," Ryan said.

"All of them?"

"Uh, yeah. I think. There were four of them."

"That's all," Jack said. "There were only four in here. We're clear."

"So, where's Stella?" Lucy asked.

*                              *                              *

Stella followed the Kazon guard into the cargo hold, staying a couple of steps behind. She watched as he checked the cartons and boxes reading the shipping labels on each. He turned to her, "There's no need to follow me," he said looking into her eyes through vertical slits characteristic of the Kazons' cat-like eyes. He dropped them to a data pad and typed on it.

"I'm following orders," Stella wondered what information he was entering on his pad. *All the cargo,* "What're you recording?" She asked.

"It's not your concern," he replied stepping to the next pen.

This continued as the guard made his way through the cargo hold recording information from each crate. Stella followed watching and becoming bored until her communicator alerted her to an incoming message, Jack came online and asked, "Where are you?"

"In hold A following the inspector," she turned her back to the guard.

"What?" Jack's voice was hard, stressed. "He's still there?"

"Yeah, why?"

"Restrain him," Jack said.

"What's going on?"

"Just do it!" Jack disconnected.

Stella turned around to find the guard gone. *Great!* Stepping ahead to the end of the aisle she turned the corner.

*                              *                              *

Jack ordered Dan and Ryan to deck six to help Stella restrain the guard. Deck six was a long corridor extending down the middle of the ship where access doors to the cargo bays A and B were located. At the front of the deck was the airlock where Bove had exited the ship and where the Kazon guards had entered. The only other thing in the corridor was the lift to the upper decks.

Dan's muscles tightened as he slipped into cargo bay A and glanced around. He was in the holding area in front of the loading dock. To his right was the docking port, and across from that was the shuttle bay. Between him and the shuttle bay was the entrance to the cargo bay which stood open inviting him into the unknown beyond.

He took a deep breath and turned to Ryan, "Back me up. We don't know what kind of weapon he has." He took another breath and stepped into the bay. The cargo bay was a series of cages enclosed with linked fencing. The pattern of cages left a path straight ahead through the bay with a connecting path to each side. Dan pointed to his right for Ryan to follow that path while he took the one straight ahead. Ryan nodded and turned to the right proceeding into the bay.

Dan moved cautiously forward keeping as quiet as possible. His hand phaser shook as he eased forward, sweat beaded on his forehead, and he could hear his heart pound in his chest. He sucked in air as silently as he could. No movement or sounds disturbed the stillness as he advanced. Each cage he checked had crates and boxes of diverse sizes, yet packed tight so no one could be hiding between or behind them. He moved from cage to cage listening for any disturbance, there was nothing.

Ryan went down the side aisle and turned the corner when he heard a slight rustle. He froze. His shoulders tightened. *I don't need this. I didn't sign up to fight, I'm a pilot*. But he had fought before while he was in the service and during his last job. It wasn't something new to him, just something he wanted to avoid. But still…

His heart pounded and his figures tightened around the phaser handle. He listened for another sound but heard nothing. Stepping to the next cage he peered in when suddenly something hit him from behind knocking him against the opposite cage with a clank of steel links. His face slammed into the pen bouncing him back. He stumbled dazed and raised his arm to protect himself. "Dan!" he shouted.

The Kazon swung at him hitting his arms and knocking his phaser from his hand. It skidded across the floor out of reach. He pushed the Kazon backing him up a couple of steps, then he kicked him throwing him against the steel fence with a loud crash.

The Kazon pushed from the pen, steading himself he raised his weapon toward Ryan ready to fire when Dan skidded around the side of the path and shouted, "Stop! I won't hesitate!" His phaser pointed at the Kazon's head.

The guard turned to look at Dan, anger flooding his face, his fur stood up on his neck and arms, and his ears twitched. He stepped back from Ryan, lowering his weapon.

Ryan picked up his phaser and pointed it at him, "Put it down," he said.

The Kazon laid his weapon on the floor keeping his eyes glaring at Dan and hissed, "You will pay for this."

Stella bolded around the corner and came to a stop when she saw the Kazon at bay. "Everyone okay?" She asked.

"We got him," Dan said. "Search him, make sure he has no more weapons, then we'll put him in that cage." He pointed to the cage next to Ryan.

Ryan searched the Kazon pulling a knife from his boot and a hand phaser from his inner pocket. Satisfied, he opened the cage and shoved the Kazon in. He slammed the door closed and engaged the lock.

"We have the intruder," Dan announced to the bridge, "he's in a cargo cage. He'll be secure there until we decide what to do with him."

"Keep an eye on him," Jack told Dan.

"I'm coming up," Stella said and headed for the bridge. When she arrived, she confronted Jack, "Now are you going to tell me what's going on?"

"They took Bove," Jack looked her in the eye, dead serious.

"Took him? Where?"

"I don't know. Dan was there," Jack said.

Her face changed from shock to anger, her arms straight down at her sides, hands in fists. She shook her head. "Shit!"

*　　　　　*　　　　　*

Zabi fired the main engines and the Dark Star lifted from the Ardonian surface. "Engage the transit drive the minute we're clear of the atmosphere," he told Luke.

"So much for revenge," Luke's voice was filled with anger.

"You'll get yours," Zabi said, "We'll find the Ibex and both of us will have our satisfaction."

"That's good for you. Bove will rot in a Kazon prison, which should make you happy, but Tom's still gone. Where's my satisfaction?"

"Don't worry, we'll find him. It may take a little time, but we'll find him. Then you can have your fun."

"I hope you're right," Luke engaged the transit drive, and the Dark Star was gone along with their anger at Tom and the Ibex.

# Twenty-Four

Two guards took Bove to a secure room, one remained to keep watch. Bove tapped his communicator and heard static, he tried again. *Must be interference.* Dan wasn't with him, and they hadn't seemed interested in him, so it was safe to assume he returned to the ship. *Good, he'll explain what happened.*

The door opened and Surton came in, "Time to leave," he said and motioned to the guard who pulled Bove to his feet. "Bring him," Surton turned and headed out.

They ushered Bove down a corridor and into a shuttle followed by the guard and Surton. The door slid closed, and they were off heading down to the planet.

"Now," Surton reached his hand out, "give me your communicator."

"Am I not allowed to let my crew know what's happened?" Bove asked.

"The communicator," Surton nodded to the guard who lowered his weapon across his lap, his finger sliding into the trigger ring.

As Bove reached to comply he said simply, "Lucy, transit," and pulled the communicator from his ear. He extended his arm towards the soldier with the communicator lying on his palm, "What's going on?" he asked.

Surton ignored him, tapped his ear, and said, "Secure the ship." He turned to Bove, 'You're clever. I'll give you that." He dropped the communicator on the floor and crushed it with his boot. "You're being held on suspicion of espionage," He looked Bove in the eye. "We don't take kindly to spying," he added.

Bove felt a shiver run through his shoulders and down his back. He took a deep breath, *stay calm*, he told himself even though panic was knocking at his mind's door. He cleared his throat. "What evidence do you have?" he choked out.

"I don't have that information." Surton turned away from Bove indicating the conversation was over.

Bove sat confused while the shuttle headed to the surface.

*       *       *

Jack was in shock that Bove was taken into custody and that they had captured a Kazon guard. He wondered what would happen next. "Can you get Bove, or at least see where he is?" he asked Lucy.

"He doesn't respond, but they put him on a transport," Lucy stopped typing and looked at Jack, "Why would they take him like that? Is he under arrest?"

"I don't know, but I'm going to find out," he started to say more but a command from the surface interrupted him shocking everyone on the bridge, *Lucy, transit.*

Lucy shook her head not sure what she heard "Did I hear that right?" She asked anyone.

"You did," Jack said, "check with Bove to verify."

"I can't raise him; I get nothing, like his communicator's off."

"Or dead," Ryan said.

"Don't even think that!" Lucy glared at him.

"We got an order," Jack interrupted, "Lucy, transit when you're ready."

"We need to be free of the dock," She turned to her console and started typing.

The com activated, "Open your airlock and prepare to be boarded. Your ship is under Kazon authority and is to remain until further notice." The voice went silent.

"Can we break the docking clamps?" Stella asked.

"What are we going to do?" Ryan's voice shook and his face went pale.

The com crackled, "You must comply immediately."

Jack pressed the response pad, "We are a free vessel under the orders of our captain. Release the docking clamps!"

"Open your airlock or we will be forced to breach it."

"Ryan, start the engines. Lucy prepare to transit. Stella, can you work the weapons?"

"Sure can."

"Activate and arm them," Jack said and looked around the bridge.

"Weapons armed and ready, what should I aim at?" Stella asked.

"Target the clamps, "Jack told her, then into the com he demanded, "Release the docking clamps!"

Silence followed his statement. Everyone held their breath, hands posed over their respective pads waiting for their next order.

"Breach in one minute. Shut down your engines!"

"One minute," Jack said. "Should we wait? Or do we take our chances?"

"Wait," Ryan said.

"Ryan," Jack turned to him, "When Stella blasts the clamps, move the ship enough to break the connection to the ramp, and make it quick."

"Thirty seconds."

Over the com, Dan said, "Take a chance, I don't want to be held by them. We need to get away."

The sound of blasters on the airlock door rang loudly from the docking bay.

"Stella fire," Jack ordered.

Things happened fast when Stella pressed the firing pad. A muffled roar rang through the ship followed by a strong shutter as the clamps snapped apart sending debris flying through the docking station. Ryan fired the thrusters moving the ship from the docking bay and disengaging the boarding ramp. The Kazon soldiers trying to breach the airlock were thrown from the ramp against the side of the ship and the walls of the bay.

"You have violated Kazon security! Do not leave the docking bay!"

"Are we clear?" Jack's voice trembled.

"Almost," Lucy said. "The air has to clear."

Ryan moved the ship farther out of the bay.

"Stop or you will be fired on!" The Kazon command demanded.

"When?" Jack looked at Lucy, then at Ryan, concern in his voice.

"Okay, now," Lucy held her hand over the transit pad ready for the order.

"Transit," Jack commanded, and Lucy's hand dropped to the pad.

The Ibex was gone leaving behind an array of destruction to the docking station and its soldiers.

The bridge was silent when they dropped out of transit. Everyone was slightly disoriented. "Where did you send us?" Jack asked.

"To the nearest star," Lucy said, "Is that too close?"

*We need to figure this out*, Jack turned to Ryan, "Ryan set an orbit around one of the inner planets."

"What's your plan?" Stella looked at him.

"What just happened?" Lucy shook her head in disbelief.

"I wish I knew," Jack said to both questions. "Any ideas?"

Lucy turned toward him, "It doesn't look good."

"Why would they arrest him?" Ryan asked.

"We don't know if he's arrested, but our prisoner said something about spies," Stella said. "They must think we're here to spy on them."

"Well, we are," Ryan said matter-of-factly.

Lucy ran her hands through her hair. "You think he's okay?"

"Don't speculate," Stella said to Lucy. "Wait until we get more facts. As far as we know nothing has happened to him, at least nothing bad."

"We don't know that," Lucy was going to say more, but Stella interrupted.

"Lucy!"

Lucy looked up into Stella's eyes and took a deep breath. "Yeah, okay."

"Can you track his vitals with sensors?" Jack asked.

Lucy shook her head trying to clear her thoughts, "Not from here. We need to be much closer."

"So, we don't know anything," Jack said. "He could be dead by now."

"Don't say that," Lucy's voice shook. "Not now."

"Or he could be fine," Stella said. "We shouldn't conclude anything until we have more information."

"I'm going to find out what happened," Jack switched the com on, "Dan, how's our captive?"

"Quiet as a dead rat," Dan shot back. "What are we going to do with him?"

"I'll be right down," Jack said. "Stella you're with me. We'll be back soon." He and Stella left Lucy and Ryan on the bridge and headed for the cargo bay.

Lucy sighed and dropped her head into her hands.

Ryan glanced at her, "I'm sure everything'll be fine." He assured her.

She looked up at him and shook her head, "I don't know," she pushed her hair from her eyes.

The intercom crackled, "Dan's headed back up there." Then it went silent.

Dan entered the bridge. "Jack and Stella are interrogating our captive," he said. "They'll find out what's going on."

*   *   *

"I'm getting tired of this," Jack glared at the Kazon. "We need to know what happened to our captain."

"We don't talk to spies." The Kazon stared at Jack, anger etching his face. "I will give you nothing."

"Why are you on board?"

The Kazon's face remained blank, his mouth closed in a tight line and his pawlike hands curled into fists. He hissed.

"Fine." Jack turned to Stella and motioned her out of the pen.

Once out of earshot, Jack asked, "What do you think? Will he break?"

"Probably not." She said, "Kazons are trained to resist interrogation. It's going to take someone much better trained at breaking prisoners than us."

"What do you suggest?"

"We hang on to him and use him to get Bove back."

"What's he talking about us being spies?"

"Don't know," Stella glanced around. "Maybe something in the cargo hold gave the wrong impression."

"Like what?"

"I don't know."

"He's going to be fine in there. I'm heading back to the bridge. We need to figure out what our next move is." Jack left. Stella looked around again, went back to the pen holding the Kazon, and made sure everything was secure, then followed Jack back to the bridge.

When she arrived, Lucy was telling Jack what she thought they should be doing.

"If we get to a moon around an outer planet, we should be close enough to pick up Bove's vitals. We'll be able to tell his condition." She looked at him with a stubborn face, eyes locked on his daring him to contradict her.

"Do you have a planet in mind?" He asked.

"The fifth planet has a large moon that will work."

"Can you get us there without being detected?" Jack asked Ryan.

"I can get us there. I don't know what tech they have in the area."

"I can keep us undetected," Lucy added.

"How?"

"I can modulate our deflectors to hide us from their sensors while we approach. They'll have to be at full power all the way in."

"Is that a problem?"

"It'll use a lot of energy, but we can replenish it later."

"And if we need it, what then?"

"It won't take all of it. We'll still have plenty left. We can do this." She added emphatically.

Jack shifted in his chair and tapped his fingers on the panel in front of him. "You're sure about this?"

"Yeah," Lucy nodded.

Jack looked at each member of the crew, then at Stella who just raised her shoulders and tipped her head. "Okay, we need to do something. Fifth planet, which moon?"

Lucy showed Jack the moon and then prepared to transit to it.

Jack set the navigation for the fifth planet and its moon, then turned to Ryan and gave the order, "Take us there."

# Twenty-Five

The guard rousted Bove up and out of the shuttle while Surton sat quietly and watched. The shuttle door closed, and it lifted off, the guard shoved Bove toward a nearby building, "Move on," he said. Bove was shoved through a door into a holding area where he was pushed into a cell and the force field activated. "Wait here," the guard told him and left.

"Like I have a choice," Bove said to the guard's back as he disappeared through a door at the end of the corridor.

Shortly another guard came and escorted Bove to an interrogation room where he was pushed down with restraints clamped around his wrists and to the arm of the chair. Two Kazon soldiers sat opposite him with grim looks on their faces. "State your name for the record." The soldier on the left opened a folder and placed his paw, pen ready, on the page.

After a few general questions, things became serious. The first soldier said, "We have information from a reliable source that you have been sent here to gather information concerning our plans for Kryth. Our planet you have illegally colonized. Is this correct?" He tapped his paw on the tabletop while studying Bove.

Bove sat stunned, thoughts running around in his head trying to produce an answer. Where could they have gotten that information? Is someone in the government working for the Kazons? Have they betrayed him? *But why?* "I am here to set up a trading agreement," he said. "I don't know where you got information that I was sent to spy, but it's incorrect."

"Is that so?" The soldier stood and motioned the other one to follow him out of the room. A couple of minutes later they returned and sat down. "We believe some time to think about your statement will help clear things up." He stood and unlocked the restraints holding Bove's hands. They hustled him up and herded him into a closed room with no windows and a solid door with a slot for food. There was a bed, of sorts, a toilet and sink, and a blanket. A single light in the ceiling lit the room.

*How long will I be here*? He wondered as the day's events began to wear on him. His mind was in turmoil with concerns about the crew and the ship. Were they able to get away? His mission was revealed to the Kazons by whom? Did they have enough information to keep him here, did they need a reason? He couldn't think anymore, what he needed was a long rest, a good sleep. Tomorrow would come too soon.

He lay down on his bunk and closed his eyes stretching his arms and legs to ease his muscles, he took several deep breaths and slowly exhaled releasing the tension from his body with the escaping air from his lungs. Sleep pushed at his mind promising peace and rejuvenation until it covered him like a warm blanket.

He sensed someone waking him and he sat up looking around. The room was pleasant with soft colors and a fresh scent filling the air; the sound of bubbling water drifted through an open window. He was no longer on Ardonia. He rubbed the sleep from his eyes wishing for something to drink.

"We must speak about your mission." Kabluff was sitting across the room studying Bove. "You remember what we discussed last time we spoke?" He asked.

Bove looked around before spotting Kabluff, "Why am I here?" He felt his face redden, his muscles tighten, and he clenched his hands into fists. "I'm done with these visions. And I'm done listening to you." He stood and looked around; the room was unfamiliar. He turned to face Kabluff.

"You have no choice. You must listen," Kabluff told him.

"Why?" Bove opened his hands stretching his fingers. "I'll do as I please, not what you demand of me."

"You must do as you committed. Do you remember your commitments?"

Bove felt Kabluff's eyes boring into him like he was reaching into his mind to see his next word. Bove hesitated, then nodded his head.

"Good."

The previous vision came flooding back into Bove's mind. He was supposed to stop the Kazons from further action against Kryth. He was to make the Kazons leave the colonists as they were. He was to make peace. "You have already told me what I must do," he said.

"Things have changed. The Kazons are planning to remove the colonists by force if Earth doesn't take action soon." Kabluff raised his arm and swept it in an arc. Before Bove was a quadrant of the galaxy showing Kryth and the Kazon empire. Stars shined like the lights of a city and Kryth stood out along with the planets of the Kazon empire.

"You see how close Kryth is to the Kazon empire? That is why they claim it, and why they are willing to confront Earth. And you, Bove, are at the center."

"I'm what?"

"You are the center of this confrontation," Kabluff repeated.

"No, no, no!" Bove's voice rose with each word. "I am only to gather information. That's all. I'm not the center of anything."

"You are the only contact, the only person that can influence their position," Kabluff said. "You have committed to helping, and this will help thousands of people. Isn't that what you want? Or…," he held Bove with his eyes, "would you prefer the bog?"

"No!" Bove felt the pressure mounting. Of course, he didn't want problems with the Kazons. He didn't want the colonists moved either. And he didn't want to return to the bog. The bog with poisoned water and dead bodies. The bog where there was no way out but through the water that would seep into your pours spreading its poison into every cell. No, he did not want to return there.

His mind spun with ideas, none of any help. The Kazons wouldn't start a war over a single planet, there would be too much to lose. It would be foolhardy! But he didn't know the Kazons, are they foolhardy, willing to lose hundreds or thousands of lives in a war? Earth had not seen a war in a thousand years. But the Kazons—have they? He didn't know. How could he confront them? *Once I'm out of here, then I can confront them about Kryth.* Then his thoughts turned back to Kabluff. "How do I know you are not lying to me? Just like you did on Kryth. How can I trust what you say?"

"You can see for yourself, but you must get free of this prison. You will see their build-up of forces.

Their new manufacturing plants for the latest weapons. Their heightened security around the planet. You don't need to trust us or believe us; you only need to see what's there."

"And if I don't get free, what then?"

"Then the galaxy will be facing war unlike anyone has ever seen. If you cannot succeed, the future will be changed forever." Kabluff looked down at his hands folded in his lap and slowly shook his head, "You must succeed. You are the only hope to stop what's coming." He looked up into Bove's eyes, searching for understanding.

Bove shook his head and looked away, a chill ran up his spine and across his shoulders causing him the shiver. He rubbed his arms to stave off the feeling.

"You know what you must do." Kabluff waved his hand again and the display vanished. "You can believe me or not, but you will see I speak the truth now that you are on Ardonia. It is up to you how you proceed, but you must confront the Kazons." Kabluff stood, stepped to the window, and stood gazing out for a moment, "It is for your future that you must do this."

"I have no way to talk to anyone. And if I do get free, I'm not staying around to talk."

"You must find a way," Kabluff said, "Now you must go."

Before Bove could utter a word Kabluff waved his hand and Bove was lying on his bunk seemingly waking from a dream. A dream he could remember every detail of. He rubbed his eyes and ran his fingers through his hair. Another vision telling him what he must do; how to go ahead with his mission. But he could not believe it. He had been lied to in his other visions and there was no reason to believe this was any different.

Thoughts circled his mind; *Richerson wants information about military capabilities and intentions, Kabluff wants me to persuade the Kazons to leave Kryth alone, and I want the visions to stop. One thing at a time.* But first, he needed to get free by convincing them he was not a spy. *They don't have proof.* He was sure they would realize that and free him shortly then he could talk to someone. Someone in the military who could see the folly of confronting Earth and be able to influence the rulers of Kazon to leave the colonists on Kryth. That seemed easy enough, he would only have to find a person interested in cesium, which would be the military.

He lay back on the bunk and closed his eyes trying to get to sleep. He had no idea what time it was, his visions tended to warp time, so he never knew how much time had passed while he was in one. *Is it early enough to still get some sleep*, he wondered as he drifted off.

# Twenty-Six

The fifth planet of the Ardonia system was a massive gas giant with twelve moons of varying sizes. Lucy picked one that was near the size of Earth and on the far side of the planet. Its gray surface panned across the main view screen as the Ibex moved into an elliptical orbit.

Stella watched the view as the surface panned by, not paying attention to the moon but thinking about the crew and the fate of Bove. The crew was inexperienced in dealing with a situation like this. She could feel the tension and knew none of them had a good handle on how to get Bove back.

Jack cut the view, "Not much to see," he said. "Cut the engines once we're stable." He told Ryan. "Dan, keep a watch for any Kazon ships, and keep the weapons ready."

"I've got the sensors ready to scan the planet," Lucy said, "but we'll have to wait until the moon's clear."

"How long?"

"Eight hours," Lucy's voice was tense.

"Can we contact him?" Jack asked.

"Not from here, the planet's blocking any signal. I could send a relay out, but it might be spotted. The last time I tried there was no connection. His com may be off."

"Or destroyed," Dan turned to Lucy.

"Why would it be destroyed?" Concern clouded Lucy's face, then realization. "Don't even think that." She scowled at Dan.

"Just saying." Dan raised his hands, palms out.

"Don't lose hope," Stella cut in. She stood up and took the captain's chair. "We need a plan," she said looking around the bridge.

"For what?" Dan glanced between her and Jack.

"Well, we need to figure out how to get him."

"I'd like to know why he's being held," Ryan turned to Stella.

"Yeah," Jack agreed.

"It doesn't matter. We need to find a way to get him back." Stella held her voice steady.

"Okay," Lucy agreed.

"So how do we get him back?" Ryan looked at Jack.

"I'm not sure," Stella watched Jack expecting him to interrupt. "We should think about it and come up with suggestions. What do you think?"

"Yeah, I guess," Jack looked at Dan and Ryan who nodded. "Lucy?"

"Sure."

"Okay," Stella stood up, pushed her hair back, and asked, "Anyone hungry?"

"Not me," Jack shook his head. Dan and Ryan agreed.

Lucy looked up with sad eyes, "I guess I should eat."

Stella smiled, "If you change your minds come on down." Then to Lucy, she said, "We'll make something delicious," and headed for the lift with Lucy close behind.

They fixed a meal working mostly in silence then sat across from each other to eat.

Lucy picked at her food, taking an occasional bite without looking at Stella.

"You're worried about Bove, aren't you?" Stella laid her fork on the plate. She watched Lucy poke at her meal.

"Yeah, I am," she said.

"Me too."

"I'm afraid to think about it. His com doesn't respond like it's not there. Like he's not there. You know what I mean?" Tears glistened in her eyes that she swiped away with a napkin.

"I know what you mean, but you can't think negative thoughts. We don't know how he is, and his com may very well be destroyed because they wouldn't want him contacting us and giving us information about where he is." Stella laid her hand on top of Lucy's.

Lucy looked up, ran her hand around the back of her neck, and gave a weak smile to Stella. "I guess you're right. I'm just being silly."

"No, no, not at all. I understand how you feel. It's easy to let thoughts of what might have happened run through your head. But when you do that things get confusing, and you start to believe the worst. We don't know anything and until we have information we shouldn't speculate."

Lucy nodded unsure if she could stop. She wanted to do something to find out if he was okay, but she understood what Stella was saying.

"Is he special in some way?" Stella asked.

"Not really," Lucy rubbed her nose and patted her eyes. "It's just before he came along, Lucus was a tyrant. He made all the decisions about what we did and didn't even tell us anything. Look at what he did to you. We didn't even know you were in the hold, well all of us but Tom." She looked up at Stella and realized what she had just said. "I'm sorry! I didn't mean to bring that up."

"It's fine. You were saying about Bove."

"Yeah, he tells us everything and lets us decide what to do. He even made us all part owners in the ship when he could have just claimed it for himself."

"I see," Stella let out a breath. "Well, eat up. We need to make plans."

Lucy smiled at her, "Thanks for listening. I don't feel right talking to the others about how I feel. Particularly, Jack, he doesn't seem to notice anything."

"I know what you mean. Men, they can get into their own heads and forget the world exists."

"Yeah, "Lucy agreed.

"You like Jack, huh?"

"Yeah, I guess I do." Lucy looked up at her realization striking her with that last question. "Like you like Bove," she said.

Stella took a bite of her meal, slowly chewed, sipped her drink, and said, "We have plans to make."

Jack came into the kitchen followed by Ryan and Dan, "I guess we're hungry after all," He pulled a chair from the table and sat, "What'd you make?"

"Gulash," Lucy said, "It's on the counter." She pointed with her fork toward the back of the room.

After the three men served themselves and settled around the table, Jack said, "We should talk to the Kazons. Explain why we've come. I'm sure…"

Stella interrupted him, "That won't work. We need something solid to convince them of anything."

"But…" Jack started to say but when he saw Stella's stare he stopped and took a breath. "I guess you would know."

"Well," Lucy said pushing her plate from her, "we'll have to break him out. Won't we?"

That's when everyone presented ideas and soon the crew decided to first use the sensors to find him. Once they knew where he was, they could devise a plan to get him back. But no one had any new ideas. They could not see a way to get to the surface, either with the Ibex or a shuttle, without being detected by the Kazons. They hadn't found a way to communicate with Bove to tell him their plans. So, they would have to land, get into the prison, find Bove, and get him out and onto the ship. All without alerting the Kazons.

"That's just not possible," Dan said.

"We could go in hot," Jack suggested, "blast our way in and out."

"Right," Dan added, "with the whole Kazon military sitting there waiting for us. We wouldn't make it past their star cruisers."

"How 'bout an escape pod with a single person? Could it slip by the security?" Ryan asked.

"Possible," Lucy said. "But how would that help? It couldn't come back. Pods are one-way vehicles."

"Could one be modified?"

"No," Dan said.

"Why not?"

"The power it would need to escape gravity is too much. We have nothing that would fit in or on it to provide that kind of power."

The room fell silent. The crew glanced at one another hoping for an answer, but nothing came.

"What if Bove got a shuttle himself?' He could fly to us. We could meet him in orbit." Dan looked at everyone, "Well?"

"How is he going to get a shuttle, and how will we know if he has one and where to meet him?" Jack stood and walked around the table. "That's no good. We need something else."

"There must be a way," Lucy said shaking her head. "There has to be a way."

"We can try trading him for the Kazon," Stella said.

"I like that," Jack said before Stella could continue.

"You think that would work?" Ryan rubbed his hands together. "We can contact them and find out."

"It's a long shot," Stella said. "But it's worth a try."

"Why do you say that?" Jack asked.

"Typically, they don't trade prisoners. They will take the loss of one soldier rather than give up their prisoner. Particularly if that prisoner is worth something. As for Bove, I don't think he would be worth losing a soldier over, but I could be wrong."

"Contact them and ask," Jack said.

"Yeah," Lucy agreed. "When we're aligned."

"When will that be?" Dan asked.

"A half-hour," Jack said.

Silence filled the room, everyone deep in their thoughts.

"Well, we have to try," Lucy broke the silence.

"Who would we talk to?" Jack looked at Stella.

"We should start with the officer that tried to retain us," Stella told them.

"Great," Jack said, "Let's get to the bridge and Lucy can contact him."

"Wait," Stella cut in. "We should interrogate the Kazon first. Find out if he knows anything about why Bove is being held."

"Didn't you and Jack do that?" Dan asked. "And he didn't tell you anything."

"Yeah," Stella admitted, "but I think it may be worth another try. In case he's changed his mind."

"Stella's right," Jack told him. "We may find there's more to it than just calling us spies. Who can interrogate him?" He looked at Stella.

"I guess I can," she said.

# Twenty-Seven

The cargo hold was quiet and chilly. Stella rolled down the sleeves of her shirt and rubbed her arms to warm them. She turned the lock on the access door to the hold and opened it. Jack followed her inside and down the pathway to where the Kazon was locked up.

He was sitting on the floor resting his back against a crate. When they came into view he pushed up to his feet and stood legs apart and locked at the knees. "Have you come to release me?" He glared at the two of them.

"Depends," Stella kept her face stoic.

"On what?"

"We have a few questions. You answer truthfully and we may consider letting you go."

"Ask your questions," he stated smartly and crossed his arms over his chest.

Jack opened a folding chair and placed it facing the pen out of reach of the Kazon. Stella sat down and looked at him, "Sit," she ordered.

He sat on the floor again glaring at her then looked up at Jack, "Are you not man enough to question me? Just like a human, let the woman ask the questions. Are you too scared?" He smirked at Jack.

"What's your name?" Stella pulled his attention back to her.

"I am Dejak, soldier first class in the Kazon military, and I will not answer your questions concerning our military."

"You just answered the first one," Stella smiled at him. Ignoring his reaction, she leaned forward getting closer to him, "You boarded this ship intending to take control, correct?"

"We were ordered to inspect the ship. I boarded under those orders."

"Why did you hide?"

"I didn't want to be captured. I was only to inspect the cargo."

"I see," Stella leaned back studying him for a moment, "Why would your commander order you to detain the ship? We are here to begin trading with your government, why would you detain us?"

"Your captain was arrested, and your ship was to be detained also. That's all I know."

"Do you know why he was arrested?"

Dejak just stared at her, "I told you everything I know."

"You did? We were considering trading you for our captain, but that depended on your cooperation, and since you have decided not to be forthcoming… Well, I guess we won't be able to trade you. Which leaves the question, what will we do with you?" She stared at him waiting for a reaction—there was none. She continued, "There have been several ideas on that point. Some are humane, and others not so if you get my drift. What would you prefer, something fast and painless, or…" Stella stood and turned to Jack, and in a voice just loud enough to be heard, said, "Will you see to it?"

Jack nodded, "Of course."

"It will be an act of war if you kill me," Dejak jumped to his feet. "You will never return home. They will hunt you down. It won't be pleasant."

"It certainly won't be for you." Stella turned back facing him, "But if you cooperate, well things could be different."

"I don't know anything," he said.

"Then what harm can come from answering my questions? You can't divulge any information if you know nothing, right?"

Dejak slowly nodded and stepped back from the grading of the cage.

Stella sat down, "So you don't know why Bove was arrested?"

"That's right," Dejak said as he slid back to the floor.

"You said you wouldn't talk to spies when we caught you. Why would you think we're spies?"

"I never said that." He glanced at Jack.

"You did," Jack said.

"So?" Stella asked.

"I didn't say that. I know nothing about spies, or why they want your ship."

"So, you're a soldier in the military." Stella changed the conversation letting the spy topic drop. "First Class, I think you said." Dejak was confused for a moment, he stood up and glanced at Jack, then back to Stella.

"Yeah."

"Is that a high rank? First Class sounds like you're important."

"Yes, it's just below Star Captain fourth class," Dejak relaxed slightly.

"Are you stationed here on Ardonia all the time?"

"Most of the time, yeah. Sometimes we go on missions."

"Yeah, keeps it exciting huh?"

"Yeah, I guess."

"Where have you been? I know when I was in the military I got to go to some exotic places, like Kryth."

Dejak looked at her, "Kryth? That's one of our planets."

"Really, I didn't know that."

"You should keep up with your government's activities. They have placed colonies there."

"Really,"

"Yeah, and the colonists will be removed. Your government knows that; we've informed them."

"You haven't removed them yet?"

"We're not ready, but we will be soon and then they'll be removed."

"Well, that's unfortunate for them. I'm sure they will find another place to go."

"If they survive," Dejak stared at her, then turned away. "They should leave on their own," he mumbled.

"Why is that?"

"They will be removed, not relocated."

"Oh, that is bad. When will you remove them?"

"I don't know, a few months, a year, but if they leave on their own it will be better."

"Will you be going there?" Stella asked.

"We don't have any orders yet."

"Well, I'm sure you'll get them." Then to Jack, she said, "We should get back to the bridge. Get working on this trade."

"That's all you want from me?" Dejak asked as Stella stood ignoring his question. He watched them leave, then lowered his head in thought.

*    *    *

Seven hours later Lucy was at her console checking the sensors. Within the hour they would align with Ardonia and be able to start scanning for Bove. She steadied her hands as they glided over the pads entering instructions for the sensor scan. She entered the location to scan, the bio-indicators to search. Physical parameters, meters above and below the surface. She was preparing to find Bove and didn't want to make a mistake that would slow down the search. The longer it took, the more likely the Kazons would detect it. She took a breath and felt her heart slow.

As the moon circled out from behind the planet, Lucy started the scan and within minutes she had results. "I've located Bove," She felt the tension release from her shoulders and a smile spread across her face. She turned to face Ryan and Dan, "I've located Bove," she repeated.

"You said that," Dan answered. "Where is he?"

"He's in a compound west of the capital one level below the surface. He's not moving, but he's alive."

"Maybe he's sleeping. It's night down there." Ryan added.

"How are we going to get him," Lucy asked.

"We're going to trade him," Jack said as he walked onto the bridge. "For the Kazon in the hold."

"Did you find him," Stella asked following Jack in.

"He's in a compound west of the city," Dan told her.

"Lucy," Jack settled into his seat, "See if you can contact the commander in the security ring. He should be able to tell us who to ask about trading their guy for Bove."

"On it," Lucy said.

"We should stay hidden until we have some confirmation about a trade," Stella told the crew.

"I have the commander coming online," Lucy said.

"This is Commander Surton," the voice was tight, controlled. "State your name and business for clearance to dock."

"Commander," Stella started but was interrupted.

"Failure to follow these instructions will result in your destruction. Is that understood?"

"Commander," Stella said with more force than she intended, "we are contacting you to propose a trade."

"State your name and business," he repeated.

"This is Stella Thorne, and we want to make a trade," Stella held her breath and glanced at the crew.

"Do you have an authorization code?" Surton asked.

"No, we want to make a trade with you," Stella repeated.

"What is your craft designation, and what trade are you talking about?"

"This is the Ibex," Stella waved her hand at the crew to keep them quiet, "and we want to trade your soldier Dejak, for our captain, Bove."

There was silence on the connection for a full minute. Then the commander spoke more quietly, "I see. But we don't trade with spies. But if you return the soldier, we will not destroy your ship. Your choice." Surton disconnected.

"Well," Stella said, "that was pretty clear. Can they know where we are?"

"No," Lucy looked at her console, "They haven't scanned the ship. They have no idea where we are."

"Good," Stella said. "Now what?"

# Twenty-Eight

The sound of prisoners hustling out of their cells kept Bove awake and turning under his blanket to shut out the sounds. He closed his eyes hoping for sleep when the force field dropped from his cell and a guard ordered, "Come with me!"

Slumber still pressed Bove's mind and he couldn't get thoughts of his vision out of his head. He turned, facing the door.

"Now!" The guard pounded his prod on the medal door frame making a loud clang and jerking Bove more awake. Bove stood and followed him out into the corridor where a line of prisoners quietly stood waiting for the next order. Guards stood every five meters or so, watching the prisoners. Bove scanned the line, there were many Kazons as well as several humans. He was wondering where the humans had come from when one caught his eye. He had to look twice but he was sure he recognized Tom toward the end of the line. *What the hell is he doing here?*

"Move!" The guard shouted. The line moved down the corridor and into a large room where chairs sat scattered in disarray. "Find a seat," the guard ordered, and everyone found a chair and turned it to face the end of the room where the head guard paced tapping his prod into his palm. Other guards placed themselves along the walls and near the exits.

"I'm Arik," the head guard said, "and, I am in charge of this holding station. You will refer to me as *Sir*. Is that understood?"

Before he could continue a Kazon prisoner made a break for the door, but a guard caught him and threw him to the floor. A second guard pressed his electric prod against the prisoner's side causing a sharp yell. The guard pulled the prod back and kicked the prisoner who let out another yell. He shouted what Bove thought were Kazon swears at the guard prompting another kick to his side. He lay silent after that.

"Disobedience will not be tolerated," Arik told the prisoners cowering in their chairs. "Any attempt to escape will land you in a two-by-two metal box. Is that understood?" His voice rose nearly to a shout, and he tapped his prod against his hand while watching the prisoners.

Bove looked for Tom and spotted him across the room. Tom saw him at the same time. A flush covered Tom's face and he turned away. Bove waited for him to look back and eventually, he did. Bove nodded and tipped his head back to show Tom they should meet. Tom nodded.

"All of you," the guard continued, "have been found guilty of high crimes and will be moved to Salax where you will spend the remainder of your sentence working in the mines." He walked around the room checking each prisoner, for what, Bove could not imagine.

When he reached Bove he stood over him for a moment not speaking. Bove felt his presents invading his personal space, he didn't dare look up, so he kept his head down looking at the floor. Arik pushed Bove's shoulder with his prod which was inactive. "You," he said, "look at me."

Bove curled his hands into fists and clenched his teeth, *Don't react*, he told himself as he lifted his head to face the guard.

"You," the guard said again, "are a spy. Is that right?"

What was Bove to do? If he said *yes*, he would condemn himself, if he said *no*, they would punish him for lying. But he was already condemned so he had nothing to lose. "That's what they say," he said.

"Yes," the guard said in a loud voice so everyone could hear him, "They say you are a spy, and they are right." He poked Bove again with his prod, this time a slight charge shot through him, just enough to remind Bove of what he experienced on Sancus. Bove jerked from the shock and held his breath. *If only we were alone*, he clamped his teeth tight to stay quiet.

The guard continued his inspection until he was back at the front of the room. He stood watching the prisoners for a couple of minutes. The room shuffled in their chairs wondering what would come next. *Are they going to make an example of someone*, Bove shivered, *of me*? He feared.

"In four days," the guard said, "we will move you. In the meantime, you will be confined to your cells with two one-hour yard breaks a day. Your meals will be provided in your cells. Good behavior will be rewarded. Bad behavior will be punished. Is that understood?" his voice rose in volume.

The prisoners nodded.

"I want to hear it!" he shouted, "is that understood!?"

"Yeah," the prisoners said.

"I said, I want to hear it!"

"Yeah!" The prisoners yelled.

He signaled the other guards who began herding everyone out toward their cells. Bove was pushed into a cell with another human. A force field activated securing them in. Bove let out a sigh and flopped onto the lower bunk. It was fusty and stained. The cell reeked of human and alien waste, and the air was thick with sour odors of old food. It felt damp. Other cell doors gave off soft hums as force fields activated locking prisoners in. Moans of disgust slowly died down as they settled. A few yelled back and forth to one another in Kazonaise trying to make conversation that Bove could not understand. Overall, it was terrible.

His cellmate had dark hair and eyes, wore what appeared to be work clothes, and was Bove's height. "I'm Bove."

"I'm," he replied. "Are you really a spy?"

Bove looked into his dark eyes, a grim look stared back at him. "No, I'm not a spy, but someone told them I am, and they believed them."

"Wow, that's rough." Steve sat down next to Bove.

"Why are you here?" Bove asked.

"Drunk and disorderly," he said.

"That's a high crime?"

"Everything's a high crime."

"Everything?"

"Yeah, they're trying to build up their military and they need workers in the mines."

"Why?"

"I don't know. What I've heard is that their military is ill-prepared to confront anyone, and they expect a conflict soon."

"A conflict? With who?"

"Don't know. It's all rumors. They expect to keep us working the mines for a couple of years."

"To build up their military?"

"Yeah, I guess."

"They must be in sad shape, militarily, to take two years to be ready for a conflict." Bove wondered how true this was. It was the kind of information he needed to take back to Earth, but he needed to verify it. Two years before they could move the colonists, or confront Earth? Either way, it would be enough to avoid a conflict, and maybe come to a compromise. And they may be able to keep the colonists on Kryth. He let those ideas settle in his head while he wondered how to verify the information.

At seven o'clock when the Kazon sun slipped below the horizon, the lights went out. Bove covered himself with the single smelly blanket and tried to get to sleep. It was a long time coming but eventually, a restless sleep took him.

The next morning the routine began with banging prods against door frames making loud clanks to wake the prisoners, then breakfast--a thick gruel, a piece of dried bread, and a cup of water--was shoved through a slot in the wall. The water was wet, everything else was foul.

"At ten you will have one hour of yard time," the announcement came over the broadcast system.

Bove sat on his bunk wondering how he was going to get out and back to the Ibex. *If I ever do.* Depression began to set in, but he had to keep it at bay. He knew the crew wouldn't give up on him and he couldn't either. He was thinking he could enlist Tom to help with an escape. With two of them, it would be more likely to be successful. They only needed a plan, but with guards everywhere and no knowledge of the routine, how could they hope to get out? But he couldn't give up, there would be a way. He knew it.

At ten o'clock the force fields deactivated all down the corridor and the guards herded the prisoners into the yard. When Bove first stepped out, the bright sun blinded him but the fresh air that filled his lungs gave him hope. He raised his face to the warmth of the sunlight while other prisoners pushed past him into the yard. Spread across the asphalt were tables that the prisoners quickly settled around.

Bove turned to a tap on his shoulder to face Tom, staring at him, a smile trying to form on his face. Bove was speechless for a moment, then he took in a breath and said, "Tom, what are you doing here?"

"It's a long story," he answered. "It's good to see a familiar face though."

"Yeah, I guess." Bove studied Tom for a moment. "How did you get here?'

"Well, like I said, it's a long story."

"I have nothing but time, so spill it."

Tom hesitated, glanced around, then looked back at Bove. "Okay," he said, "Let's find a table." They sat facing each other, "When I left Earth," he started and told Bove everything that happened, finishing with, "I was sure Zabi would toss me out the airlock or worse when we left."

Bove felt his face heat, his fists tightened, and he took a deep breath trying to control his desire to pelt Tom. Instead, he said, "So, Zabi told them I'm a spy?"

"Yeah, I guess so." Tom slid back on the bench, glanced around, then repeated, "Yeah."

"If we weren't here…" Bove let it trail off not wanting to cause a fight but wanting to throttle Tom for giving up his plans. "So why are you telling me this? What do you want?"

"I figure we can find a way to get out of here. Together." Tom glanced at Bove, then looked quickly away. "I'll help you get out. Get free."

"How are you going to do that?"

"I have a key to open the cells. I feel I owe you that."

Bove held his surprise at bay by keeping his face stoic, "Yeah, you do," he said inwardly smiling. "And you're right, you will help me escape. But you're still off the ship, you got that?"

"Yeah, sure," Tom nodded, three times.

"Okay. So, do you have any idea how to get out of here?"

"I'm thinking we could overpower a guard and take a shuttle. Get off the planet and away."

"You think they will just let us fly a shuttle away? We'd never make it past the security ring. And there's more than one guard. We would have to take out three or four at least. You think we can do that?"

"Well, we can try..." Tom clasped his hands in his lap and shrugged his shoulders. "I don't know, just an idea. Do you have any?"

"Yeah, we'll overpower the guards, steal a shuttle, and have Ibex fly interference for us to get us away."

"You're in contact with the ship?"

"I'm sure they're out there and when we have communications, I'll tell them where to meet us."

"How are we going to overpower the guards?'

"We'll enlist some help. Do you know any of the other prisoners?"

"A couple."

"Will they help us?"

"Maybe, but we'll have to take them with us."

"Of course," Bove agreed. "Give me a day to look things over. I'll see what the guard's routine is and how to get out of here, and if a shuttle's around."

"I think they will use one to transfer us. How else are they going to move us?"

"Well, I guess we'll see. We'll talk at the next yard time." Bove got up and walked away nonchalantly.

For two days, they gathered enough information to make their plan seem possible. They recruited three others--Steve, Mike, and Raymond—all three humans. The break would be at night when fewer guards were around, and darkness would cover them. One day remained before being transferred to the mines, so a shuttle should arrive soon. Tom would release the force fields with his key, they would overpower the guards and seize the shuttle. Then they had to get off the planet. Bove was sure he could raise the Ibex and get picked up; they would only have to avoid getting blown apart before the ship could reach them. A minor problem.

There were too many flaws in the plan for it to work, but Bove knew they had to try. If they didn't do something it would be years in the mines. Death from a failed escape was better than slavery in the mines for a lifetime. He just hoped the others felt the same. He went through the plan again. The shuttle would arrive, and they would overpower a guard or two, or more, take the shuttle, then hail the Ibex and rendezvous. What could go wrong?

He wondered where the Ibex was.

Unable to communicate with the crew he had no way of knowing if they were close by. They could be light years away. If he could not contact them, their plan was sure to fail, but everyone knew the risks and they would go when the shuttle arrived. They all had to be together and committed.

He reviewed the plan with Steve who had no new input. Tom said he would discuss it with Mike and in the morning, they would review it with Raymond. If anyone thought of something they would relay it via the yard time, then in the cells. Their plan was finalized but there was no sign of a shuttle. If it didn't appear before tomorrow night, they would have to try to escape during daylight. A sure recipe for failure.

Bove turned in his bunk, *tomorrow night we go.* Once out of their cells, getting outside should be easy, the station wasn't big. They had been moved around the prison many times before being put into their cells and had a good idea of the layout. Once out they would get the shuttle and he would fly them to freedom. He'd have to figure out how to fly a foreign craft, and then get them off the planet without being shot down. That kept him awake most of the night with no solution coming to mind. *A solid plan,* he assured himself as sleep finally came.

# Twenty-Nine

A shuttle arrived during their afternoon yard hour and sat in plain view of the prisoners. Bove knew that was the way off the planet if they could get to it. He was sure their plan was solid, at midnight there would be few guards, and with five of them overpowering one should be easy, at least that's what he told himself.

The plan called for Tom to open the cells with his magnetic key, and the five of them would take out the guard closest to the shuttle and take the shuttle to freedom. Simple and straightforward, the best of plans. Bove lay on his bunk trying to calm his nerves but soon he was drifting off, his eyes sliding closed despite his anxiety.

He was outside his cell, Tom was there, down the corridor. A guard stood in front of him padding his prod against one hand. "You're not going anywhere," the guard said.

"What about Tom?" Bove glanced down the corridor.

"He's gone. I can't get him."

Bove looked again, but Tom wasn't there.

"I have you." The guard tapped his prod against his hand again. "Do I have to use this?" he asked.

Bove backed into his cell and fell onto his bunk.

*What time is it?* he stirred and opened his eyes. For a minute he couldn't believe their plan had failed, but he slowly realized it was a dream. Tom hadn't come yet, so they were still good to go. He heard a slight tap on the cell door then the force field dropped, Tom was standing in the hallway. "Come on," he whispered waving his hand for them to come.

Bove nudged Steve awake, "It's time," he said softly.

Steve stirred and sat up, blurrily eyed, but remained silent. He looked at Bove, then Tom and Mike. "Oooh," he whispered.

Bove stepped into the hallway. Behind Tom was Mike looking nervous. "Where's Raymond?" Bove asked.

"Eighteen," Tom said.

"What about his cellmate?"

"The Kazon?" Tom turned quickly heading down the hallway away from the exit door.

"We'll take him with us," Bove said following him.

"No," Mike said, "leave him. I wouldn't take one of them with us."

Bove stopped and turned to face Mike, "You are not in charge here," Bove said staring straight into Mike's eyes, "and you will do as I say, or we will leave you. Do you understand?" Bove's stare did not waver.

Mike swallowed and took a step back, "Tom…" he started.

"Tom has no say," Bove stated. "Do you understand?" He repeated.

Mike nodded in submission.

When Tom opened Raymond's cell, he quickly stepped out followed by the Kazon. "What is this?" the Kazon demanded too loudly.

"Be quiet, you're coming," Bove said to him.

"I'm not going anywhere with humans," he said folding his arms over his chest and glaring at Bove and the others.

Bove stepped so close to him he could feel his breath on his face and in a low calm voice he said, "There are five of us. Do you think you can stop us?"

The Kazon took a step back looking at all of them. He opened his mouth to say something, but Bove stopped him. "Don't!" He said. "You're already involved with an escape attempt. How do you think the guards will handle that?"

The Kazon didn't respond.

"This way," Bove said and turned back the way they had come. They followed rapidly down the hallway herding the Kazon in front as Bove led them to the door heading out of the cell block. He stopped them and tried the door. It was locked, He motioned Tom to come forward to release the lock. Bove pushed the door open a crack and peered out. A guard sat a short way down the corridor, his head hung down. He was dozing and not looking in Bove's direction. Bove noticed his prod lying across his lap, and his arms crossed over his chest. *Okay*, he eased the door farther open and slipped through it. He stood still watching the guard. There was no reaction, so Bove quietly moved toward him and when he was less than two meters away, he suddenly jerked awake. He looked to his left away from Bove then started to turn.

Bove froze for an instant then charged the guard. Just as he made his move Steve and Tom burst out of the door and all three pounced on the guard. He didn't have a chance to make a sound before he was out cold. They cut his shirt up, bound his arms and legs, and gagged him then they put him back through the door they came from.

They headed on past the control room where they crouched under the window and continued. No one had even stirred inside; it was like they were all asleep. When they reached the door to the outside Bove once again peeked out. Two guards stood next to the shuttle, both with their backs to the doorway. He turned to the others grabbed Raymond by the arm and whispered to him, "We are going to take the guards out." Then held up his hand, palm facing the others and fingers spread signaling them to stay.

Slowly they eased the door open, stepped out, and let Tom stop it from closing. Quietly they crossed the space from the doorway to the shuttle. Neither guard heard them until they were within a meter when one turned glancing back. The minute he saw them he raised his prod and lunged. Bove was quick, he twisted to the side so the prod missed him. He grabbed the guard's wrist and pulled him forward. As he came off balance Bove slammed his fist into his nose, then quickly before the guard could utter a sound, he punched him hard in his solar plexus. The guard gasped for breath unable to shout for help. Bove twisted the prod from his hand saying a silent prayer of thanks that Kazon's physical makeup was like a human's. He whipped the prod across the guard's head dropping him to the ground.

In the meantime, Raymond had rushed toward the other guard and shoved him into the side of the shuttle stunning him enough to grab his prod. Raymond tried to take it from him, but he held tight and brought it up into Raymond's side. "Owwww" Raymond shouted and fell to the ground. The guard pushed the prod into his side again and held it there until Raymond stopped moving.

Seeing what happened, Bove immediately rushed him and hit him with enough juice to silence him. He fell against the shuttle dazed and speechless, the shock wasn't enough to knock him out. Bove grabbed his collar and pulled him to his feet. "One word and you die," he said into the guard's face holding the prod to his neck.

Tom was there working on the shuttle door which quickly slid open. Mike and Steve shoved the Kazon prisoner into the shuttle, then gathered up Raymond and hauled him in. Bove followed, pushing the guard in after them and Tom came in last, closing the door. Steve got Raymond seated and strapped in. Then he and Mike pushed the guard into a seat and sat on either side of him, the prod pressed against his side. The Kazon prisoner sat across from them.

"Who's going to fly this thing?" Mike asked.

"I will," Bove dropped into the pilot's seat.

"You know how?" Steve buckled himself in.

"I'll figure it out," Bove started flipping switches and pushing buttons, Tom sat next to him as navigator.

"Tom, see if you can raise the Ibex, and tell them they need to transit here armed and ready." Bove studied the console.

"Will do," Tom flipped the communications on.

"I hope you figure it out quickly," Steve's voice was shaky. "It won't take long for someone to discover the guards aren't responding."

"Yeah, Yeah," Bove answered as he fired the engines.

"We have this one's communicator," Mike said. "If they call, we'll have our companion answer," He turned to the Kazon prisoner holding the communicator towards him, "Can you do that?"

The Kazon nodded, a sour look on his face.

# Thirty

Lucy contacted Commander Surton again and switched communications to Stella.

"I have a request in for the commander," Stella said and waited for an answer.

"This is Commander Surton, who am I speaking to?"

"We spoke previously about trading your soldier for our captain," she said, "and we want to revisit that subject."

"Ah, yes," Surton said, a smile in his voice. "So, you do. I thought I was clear that we don't trade with spies."

"You were, but we're not spies, your information is incorrect, and we have goods we think you would be willing to trade for." Stella waited for a reaction. She had a feeling that they wouldn't consider a trade no matter what she offered, yet she still hoped. She was not willing to lose Bove. Her shoulders tightened as she held her breath waiting for an answer.

"What do you have to offer?" Surton asked.

"Your soldier and cesium," Stella said.

"How much cesium?" he quickly asked.

Stella's hope rose with that question. There was a chance they could make a deal. "A thousand kilos," she said and held her breath.

"I'll need to see it before I agree. You can dock in the security ring for inspection."

"I don't think so. You'll have to meet us in a shuttle."

There was silence on the communicator. Stella looked at the crew. No one said a thing.

"Where?" Surton asked.

Stella let out her breath and smiled, giving a thumbs-up to the crew. "In orbit around the third planet. Bring Bove."

"It will have to be tomorrow," Surton said. "It will take some time to get Bove cleared. Paperwork, you know."

"Well make sure you do it."

"Of course," Surton said and disconnected.

"Can we trust him?" Dan asked.

Stella turned to the crew, "Of course not. He'll probably show up with an army prepared to take the ship and all the cargo. He certainly won't bring Bove."

"So, what good is a meeting?" Ryan looked dejected. He had almost given up getting Bove back.

"The commander of the security ring will be gone when we arrive there. We will make demands that require his approval which can give us time to locate Bove and send a shuttle to get him."

"We can't go to the security ring," Dan said. "They'll secure us with docking clamps and board the ship. We won't have a chance to request anything."

"And do you think it will be easy to just go down there and get him?" Jack asked. "He's in prison. There will be guards and locks, and who knows what else."

"Do you have a better idea?" Stella snapped, her voice rose, "Do any of you have any ideas?" She glared at everyone. The bridge was silent.

"Let's at least get to their moon," Lucy said. "We'll be close enough to move fast if the opportunity presents itself."

"It's suicide to go in like that," Jack's voice was controlled and quiet. "There must be a better way."

"What?" Stella turned to him, her lips were tight, and her eyes narrowed.

"I don't know but give it another day," Jack stood his ground and stared Stella straight in the eye.

"Another day may be too late." She turned to Lucy, "Is there any change in his routine?"

"No, just the same. Twice a day they move to the outside of the complex, then back in. The same as the last three days."

Stella leaned back in the captain's chair, "Damn!"

"Yeah," Lucy agreed.

Which moon should we go to?" Jack asked Lucy.

"The larger one."

"Do it, Ryan." Jack said, "Set a transit to the larger moon and get us there."

*        *        *

They landed on the back side of the primary moon and Lucy sent a cloaked relay to keep it undetected but allow them to listen and look at the surface of Ardonia. They would be good there for a couple of days before the moon turned toward the planet.

"What'll we do now?" Ryan asked.

"Wait," Stella said. "Let's get some sleep. Tomorrow we may have to leave, one way or another."

While grumbling the crew headed for their cabins knowing they needed rest.

Twelve twenty in the morning, planet time, an alarm went off. Lucy shot out of her bunk and headed for the bridge, the rest of the crew and Stella met her.

"What happened?" Stella asked.

"A change in the routine," Lucy said as she checked the monitor. "Bove and six others have left the complex and boarded a shuttle. It's lifting off."

"Are they being transferred?" Stella asked.

"I don't know what they're doing," Lucy said.

"We have to meet them,' Jack said.

"We don't know where it's going," Dan remarked. "We can't just blast down there unannounced."

"No, but we can get in orbit and see what's going on," Stella said.

"We can be in orbit in fifteen minutes," Ryan said.

"Do it," Stella told him.

"Is it safe?" Lucy asked.

"It better be," Stella said.

"Do it, Ryan," Jack commanded.

# Thirty-One

"Any luck?" Bove asked Tom.

"Communications are blocked," Tom tapped the console with a finger, "and if I try again, they could intercept them and know what we're up to."

"Damn!" Bove shook his head. "Hold on it's all or nothing."

He lifted the shuttle off the ground and headed for orbit. The minute he was a thousand meters up, a radio message came into the cabin. "This is Security Command; we show no flights scheduled at this time. State your destination and business."

Bove turned to the Kazon, "You,' he said, "get up here and give them what they need to let us proceed."

Mike and Steve pushed the Kazon up and toward Bove. He stumbled into a seat behind Bove, "You give us away and you're dead, understand?"

The Kazon nodded, "This is Colonel Kup, we are making a prisoner transfer."

"The transfer isn't supposed to go until tomorrow morning. Who authorized this transfer?"

"Captain Eliker," Kup said.

"Let me verify that with him before I give you clearance to proceed."

"Sir, Captain Eliker is currently unavailable and has left me in charge. I am following his orders, sir."

"Unavailable?"

"Yes sir."

There was silence from the security ring for a moment, then, "Where are you transferring them?"

"To Saltax, sir"

"Very well, you may proceed."

"Okay," Bove said, "how do we get there?"

"You'll need to proceed into orbit, it's on the other side of the planet."

Bove motioned with his head to take Kup back to his seat and keep him quiet. Then he headed the shuttle up to orbit.

"What'll we do once in orbit?" Tom asked.

"I guess we'll make a break for it. Will this transit?' he asked Kup.

"You think those star cruisers will let us by?" Steve asked.

"No," Kup said, "it'll reach an eighth light speed in seconds."

"That will have to do," Bove said and increased the shuttle's speed. They shot up past the security ring heading toward the moon in seconds.

"Shuttle," the security cut in, "You have violated the security ring. Return to orbit or you will be destroyed."

"We had a malfunction," Bove answered.

"Who is this," came the reply.

"Oh shit!" Tom slammed his hand into the console, "They're going to shoot us down!"

Bove motioned Kup back to him, "Tell um."

"It's Colonel Kup, sir. We have a malfunction with the thruster. We will have it corrected shortly."

"Bove," another communication came in. "Head around the moon we'll pick you up."

"Stella? Where did you come from?"

"Never mind just get around the moon."

"Will do. Tom get us on the moon's far side."

"On it," Tom said.

A Kazon fighter came alongside the shuttle and opened a channel of communication, "I will escort you back to the security. Change course immediately!"

Bove switched the main viewer to display the fighter. He thought about his options. Try to outrun the fighter or surrender and follow it back to the security dock to be captured again. "We have lost our guidance control and I have to loop around the moon to return to security."

"Change course as ordered or I will open fire. Understood?"

"Our guidance control…"

"That's nonsense, I saw you change course moments ago. Your guidance control's working correctly. Change course now!"

"Acknowledged," Bove said.

"Now what?" Tom asked.

"Don't go back," Mike shouted. "They'll kill us for escaping. Don't go back!"

"They'll kill us if we don't," Steve interjected. "What choice do we have?"

"One," Bove said. He spun the shuttle around directly at the fighter and closed on it.

The fighter pitched to the right, up and over the shuttle, "What're you doing?" the pilot screamed into the communicator.

"Changing course as you requested," Bove said, and at once shot around the moon's far side. It took a moment for the fighter to follow, but when he circled the moon, the shuttle was approaching the Ibex.

"I have their ship in my sights," the fighter pilot radioed to the security ring, I need backup now!" he demanded. He triggered his laser to target the shuttle and fired.

The shuttle control panel showed the weapon lock, Bove turned down and to the left. The laser missed, but it hit the Ibex in the cargo bay. Bove went past the Ibex's underside away from the shuttle bay.

A laser beam fired from the Ibex and hit the fighter in the engine compartment. The fighter swerved out of control and began to drop toward the moon when the engine cut off.

Three more fighters came around the moon spreading out in a line.

"Bove," Stella shouted, "Get in here!"

The shuttle bay door slid open. "I'm on the wrong side, I can't see the bay."

The Ibex swung around as the deflectors popped into place. Laser fire from the fighters ricocheted from the shields as they sped past the Ibex. A star cruiser came around the moon's edge turning so its main plasma guns would line up with the Ibex.

"Bove?" Stella's voice was on the edge of panic.

The Ibex stopped turning and the shuttle bay lined up with the shuttle.

The fighters turned heading back toward the Ibex. Lasers fired from the Ibex diverting the fighters to target it instead of the shuttle. The fighters razed the deflectors with lasers depleting energy.

"Hold on," Bove said as he turned the shuttle towards the Ibex. He fired the engines sending the shuttle quickly toward the bay door.

"You're going to crash!" Mike yelled.

"Slow down, you're going too fast!" Steve shouted.

"Oh shit, we're going to die!" Tom said.

An instant later Bove cut the engines and fired the retro thrusters slowing the shuttle as it entered the bay. The fighters screamed past, lasers cutting into the deflectors as the star cruiser fired its plasma guns. An instance of pain flashed through the crew of the Ibex.

Space rippled and bubbled in turmoil from the plasma bursts then the energy dissipated leaving emptiness where the Ibex once was.

# Thirty-Two

"I fear Bove's mission has failed," Kabluff said to Tanka. "There's nothing more to be done."

"Have you been able to sense him?" Tanka asked.

"No," Kabluff shook his head.

"Then I believe you are right." Tanka nodded in agreement.

"We must focus on the colony and the Kazons."

"Yes," Tanka stood and looked out the window at the city spread out below them. "How long do you think we have?"

"Maybe a year," Kabluff looked up at Tanka. "The colonists haven't started to explore the planet and it'll be another few months before they are established enough to branch out."

"And when they do, will they find the mines?"

"Of course they will. They may be hidden but with their technology, they'll spot them quickly, and once they do that they'll investigate." Kabluff took a deep breath. "The only way to stop them is to remove the colony."

"Yes, but will the *troika* agree?"

"Good question," Kabluff tapped his fingers on the arm of his chair.

"Perhaps if we tell them to let the Kazons be left to their own pursuits..." Tanka turned looking at Kabluff, arms out and hands spread open.

"No, that's not an option. They move too slowly and by the time they're ready to do anything the humans will stop them. The council wants action but no conflict and without Bove to intercede, we must see to the removal of the colony." Kabluff's tapping increased.

"That'll be our next step," Tanka sat and placed his hand over Kabluff's stopping his tapping. "We must take things one at a time."

Kabluff nodded.

"We'll figure this out. It will be okay."

Kabluff nodded again. "Thank you," he said and ran a hand over his head. The next phase of their plan to keep the crystals secure was incomplete. Many questions remained and time was running short. *How long before the colonies begin to explore in depth? How long before they discover the mines and the crystals? How long?* Kabluff dropped his head into his hands. *Too soon.*

"We must speak with the council," Tanka said softly watching Kabluff.

"Not until we have a solid plan," Kabluff shook his head, "No, we must present a good option before facing them."

"Okay," Tanka leaned back in his chair. "What's our next step?"

"Without a resource, we're limited in our options," Kabluff looked down at his hands lying in his lap. "Perhaps we could train another resource."

"Are you sure we need one?" Tanka leaned toward Kabluff, his eyes focused on him, his voice low and serious, "Could he just be out of range?"

"Possible, but not likely," Kabluff shook his head in despair.

# Thirty-Three

In the vast void between stars, space is silent and still as the tombs of Earth. A lifeless nothingness where no earthly creature can exist, but in this abyss a ripple appeared, then bubbles tumbled together pulling particles into groups that instantly formed atoms and molecules then structures that became the Ibex.

A dark void covered the main viewer. Jack glanced at it wondering where he was and gridded his teeth as the pain vanished. Reality quickly returned. "Close the shuttle bay door," he ordered.

"Done," Dan answered.

"I'm picking up seven life signs," Lucy looked at Jack.

"I thought you said there were six of them," Stella said.

"Six plus Bove," Lucy clarified.

"Dan," Jack ordered, "you and Ryan get down there and see who came aboard."

Dan and Ryan headed for the shuttle bay.

"Where did you send us?" Stella asked.

"Far away from Ardonia," Jack glanced at her.

"Yeah, but where?'

"B sector." Jack tapped a couple of pads on his console. "Report," he said to the shuttle bay.

"Bove here, we have an injury. Is Ryan coming down?"

"Yeah," Jack nodded to himself.

"We have a few others with us," Bove announced.

"Who?" Jack glanced at Lucy, then at Stella.

"A Kazon guard we had to take with us and five other prisoners that helped with the escape. One's a Kazon. We'll be up there as soon as things are under control."

*　　　　*　　　　*

Dan and Ryan rushed into the shuttle bay, spotted the Kazon shuttle, and hurried inside. Bove and a couple of others were kneeling over someone stretched out in one of the seats. Suddenly Tom stood up and turned when Dan and Ryan entered. Dan froze, shock flashed across his face and his breath caught in his throat.

"Hi," Tom said.

Bove stood and turned facing Dan and Ryan. "Ryan," he said, "Raymond needs your help. He was stunned."

"How bad is it?" Ryan asked.

"It knocked him out."

Dan cut in, "What's he doing here?"

*　　　　*　　　　*

On the bridge, they had been listening to the exchange.

"What was that about?" Lucy asked.

"Don't know," Jack said.

"Who's *he*?" Stella pressed the com pad, "Shuttle Bay, what's going on?"

"We will be up there in a few," Bove answered.

Minutes later Bove came onto the bridge followed by Tom and the others.

Stella stared at Tom, then turned to Bove, "What is he doing here?" She demanded glaring at him. "I thought…"

"Stop!" Bove said more forcefully than he intended, looked around the bridge at the crew, and then to Stella he calmly said, "Get out of my chair."

"Yes sir." She slid out and took Tom's.

"He's not here to stay," Bove checked everyone. "He helped us escape. In fact, if he hadn't been there, we wouldn't have gotten out. So, I owe him the courtesy of a ride to another port. That and nothing more. Is that understood?"

The crew nodded. "And who are they?" Jack asked, nodding towards the others standing behind Bove. The three humans in addition to Tom shuffled their feet unsure of their position.

Bove introduced everyone saying they were going to Earth also. "Dan," he said, "show them the cabins they can use while on board. It may be a bit cramped," he explained, "but it will have to do."

"Where are the Kazons you brought with you?" Stella asked.

"We put them in a cargo pen. They should be good there til we get home."

"We have another one down there also," Stella told him.

"Great, any more and they'll outnumber us." He sighed.

Dan took the newcomers and Tom to get them settled.

"I'm going to clean up and rest. Jack set us on a course to Earth, transit to the system's edge. We'll go slow the rest of the way. That'll give us time to figure things out."

Jack nodded.

*        *        *

After Bove cleaned up and rested a bit he returned to the captain's office off the bridge. He switched on the communicator, "Jack, bring Stella to the captain's office." Moments later Jack and Stella came in. "Have a seat," Bove smiled at Stella, then turned to Jack. "So, any news?'

"Not much, we avoided capture by the Kazons, twice, and saved you. But other than that, nothing to report."

"Our Kazon prisoner has been quite forthcoming with information," Stella added.

"He has? What'd he have to say?" Bove was surprised and pleased. He smiled.

"Well," Stella continued, "he told us the Kazons are trying to build up their military. It seems they aren't prepared to engage anyone at the moment. They plan to remove the colonists from Kryth once they have their military improved."

"And how long is that going to take?"

"He didn't say."

"Jack, get him and the guard we brought together with Kup, let's see what they have to say to each other. Record everything that goes on between them."

"Kup?" Jack asked.

"Yeah, the prisoner that came with us."

Jack nodded and left.

Bove looked at Stella, "You look good," he said, *really good.* She smiled and lowered her head, then glanced up at him. He looked away, "So you got him to talk…"

"Are you taking me back home?" She asked.

"Is that where you want to go?"

"I'd like to see this through to the end," she let her fingers wrap around the arm of the seat. "But, if I'm in the way…"

"No, no, you're not in the way," Bove quickly interrupted. "Not at all." He looked around the office at nothing in particular then his eyes came back to her. She was staring right at him, and a smile curved her lips.

"So," she said, "I guess I'm here for the duration."

"Are you comfortable in your cabin?"

"Yeah, why?"

"Oh, nothing," he glanced away, "I just want to be sure my guests are comfortable," he said looking back at her.

"And, if I'm not?" she asked with coquetry.

"Well, I guess there would have to be some changes," He felt his face warm and suppressed a smile then glanced over her head and anywhere other than her brown eyes that so captivated him. "But you're comfortable."

"Yes." She smiled.

"Very good." He looked back at her, straightened in his chair, and laid his hands on the desktop. He cleared his throat, "I need to talk with Lucy."

"Of course," Stella stood to leave.

"I'll see you later?"

Stella nodded with another smile and left.

Bove sat for a couple of minutes wondering about what had just happened. He cleared his head not wanting to think about it and asked Lucy to join him.

She arrived in minutes and sat across from him, "I'm glad you're back," she said.

"Yeah, so am I," he frowned, then asked. "Were there problems?"

"Not really, Stella kind of took over, but Jack kept her in line."

"That's good. You think it was a good experience for him? He needs to be able to run the ship while I'm gone."

"Are you leaving again?"

"I don't plan to, but you never know."

"Yeah," she gave a slight smile and looked down at her lap.

"Well, did you get a chance to think about my visions?" He asked. That was the real reason he wanted to talk to her. She was sharp, well-educated, and knowledgeable in many areas. That's why he had confided in her, now he hoped she had figured out his visions and how to stop them.

"I haven't had a lot of time to really get into the details, but I have an idea."

"Well, anything will help. I want to stop them or control them. Do you have any idea how to do that?"

Lucy nodded, excitement glowing on her face, "I think I know how they work. How the people that are giving you the visions are doing it." She paused for a moment and glanced around at Bove's desk, "You may find this hard to believe and think I've got a loose screw or something."

"No, just tell me what you think," he leaned towards her, eyes focused on her.

"Okay, here goes. I think they are controlling time and space, well time."

"What?"

"Hear me out, okay?" She stopped and looked at Bove waiting for him to acknowledge.

He nodded.

"You said in your vision on the three hills you were hurt. Fractured arm and foot, or something like that?"

"Yeah."

"Well, it takes at least six weeks for a fracture to heal, right?" Bove nodded listening. "And when you woke from the vision no time had passed, you said it was the same night, right?"

He nodded again, "The next morning."

"Right, so how could you have healed that quickly?" Before Bove could answer, she continued, "You couldn't have. You had to be gone for six weeks or so. Now, if you were gone six weeks it couldn't have been the next morning, so time must have stopped on the ship while you were on the three hills." She smiled, nodding her head as if she agreed with herself. "Time must have stopped on the ship for six weeks while you healed. Are you with me?"

Bove looked bewildered, his mouth was open ready to say something, but he couldn't quite think of what to say. What she had said made sense even though it didn't. She went on, "Also you were in a different place—the three hills. How did you get there? The visioners moved you there from the ship."

"How?' he asked, still trying to catch up to her line of thinking. He hadn't quite accepted the time-stopping thing, yet he couldn't think of another explanation. It all seemed like science fiction.

She continued, "If they can be out of phase with time, they could have boarded the ship and taken you to the three hills, left you there for six weeks so your injuries could heal, then put you back on the ship and started time again." She watched Bove as he tried to accept her explanation, wonder flickering across his face and disbelief creasing his brow. "Were you asleep on the three hills any time?"

"Huh? Uh, yeah. I kind of dozed off at the temple gates, but not for long. I knew I had to finish the path in a single day."

"More like in six weeks," Lucy added. "You must have slept for days at a time at those gates. Did you feel better when you left them?"

"Well, yeah. I had a rest and water to boost my energy."

"Really? Water and rest to boost your energy? You were hurting and tired and a short rest and a drink of water is not going to help that much."

"Hum," Bove thought about all she had told him. "If you're right… What other explanation do you have?'

"None," She leaned forward, "You had to be gone six weeks at least. There's no other way you could have healed. You do understand that?"

"Yeah, I do." He still looked bewildered. Yet he nodded his head as he thought about it. Finally, he stopped, rubbed his hand through his hair, and sat back in his chair, "So, can we stop them?"

"I don't know. At least we understand what's happening during your vision. Whenever you are when you have a vision, time will stop for everyone, and they won't notice anything. When time starts again, they will pick up right where they were."

"Well, that's something." Bove shook his head still trying to absorb everything. "I guess that makes sense when you think about it. But, still, it doesn't seem possible," he shook his head. "Do you think you can stop them?"

"I'll work on it. I can't be sure, but I do have a couple of ideas."

Bove nodded at a loss for words. Lucy's explanation made sense, yet it seemed impossible. He tried to accept what she had told him, but he was still doubtful.

# Thirty-Four

Six days after reaching the outer rim of the Sol system they approached Earth and made contact. They were directed to a landing pad near the capital. Back where it all began. Bove was to meet with James Richerson at his earliest convenience, which meant as soon as possible. He asked Stella to go with him.

He had directions to a government building close to the capital, third-floor room C5. At the table sat the same five men he remembered from the first meeting. A cart with refreshments sat in the corner. He introduced Stella, then helped himself to a pastry and coffee. Stella declined any, and they took seats opposite James Richerson.

"So," James said, "how did your mission go?"

"Not so good," Bove felt his shoulder muscles tighten and his fingers curl into fists, Stella lay her hand on his forearm. He took a breath and let it out slowly, "I was arrested and thrown in prison."

"What?" Butler almost shouted, "They threw you in prison?" He stood and turned around, "I can have a division in place in two days," he said to Richerson, "Two days." He repeated.

"Calm down, Bo," Richerson said.

"They put him in jail," Rage covered Butler's face, as it flushed red, and a vein stood out on his forehead.

"Let him finish," Pencaster gave Butler a sharp look. Butler sat back down, anger still flaring on his face.

"Continue," James said to Bove and glanced at Stella.

"We did get some information," Bove looked at Butler.

"Go on," James prompted.

"The Kazons are in the process of rebuilding their military," Bove looked around the room to get a feel of the reaction. Butler appeared unhappy, still angry, and wanting to do something. Walter Mitchell and his assistant Eric remained calm listening. Pencaster looked back expecting more from Bove, as did James.

"What are their intentions," Butler seemed to have calmed down.

"They're a few years from having a military capable of engaging with us" Bove continued. "Stella actually got this from one of the Kazons we brought back."

"You brought Kazons here?" Butler sounded surprised.

Bove nodded.

"Well, where are they? We need to interrogate them at once."

"We have them in a safe place," Stella glanced around the table.

"Bo," Richerson said looking at Butler, "there's time."

Butler sat back with a scow on his face and arms crossed over his chest.

"Go on," Richerson turned to Bove.

"Well, they're building up their military. And they claim Kryth is in their territory, and they have the right to remove the colonists."

"We know that," Pencaster said.

"Over my dead body," Butler added.

"Bo," Richerson looked at Butler, who leaned back in his chair with a huff.

"There's more to it than that," Bove continued. "They indicated they would remove them. Not relocate them."

"Remove them? What do you mean?" Pencaster asked concern crossing his face.

"It sounds like they intend to get rid of them. Permanently." Bove said.

"Well, that puts a different spin on things," Pencaster said. "We will have to consider that in our planning.

"Why were you arrested?" Richerson wondered aloud.

"They thought I was a spy," Bove said.

"What did you say to make them think that?" Pencaster sounded accusing.

"I didn't say anything. They arrested me the minute we docked." Bove leaned back in his chair, "Someone ratted me out."

"Who?" Pencaster looked at each of the others. "Not one of us." It was a statement of fact.

"Does someone have it out for you?" Richerson leaned towards Bove, a serious look in his eyes. "We can take care of him for you."

"What does that mean?" Bove glanced at Pencaster.

"Have him arrested."

"For what?" Bove wondered how far they would go for him.

"For interfering with a mission of national security. He is from Earth, right?"

"I don't really know, but I can handle him myself." Bove waved his hand to dismiss the whole affair. He didn't want to have any problems with the colonies if Zabi wasn't from Earth. And, if he did meet up with him again, he would take care of it himself. He didn't need Earth looking after him like a big brother. That would put him in more danger, and he didn't need that. "You don't need to worry about it."

"Very well," Richerson turned to Pencaster. "What would you recommend at this point, Arnold?" he asked.

"Well," Pencaster looked at Butler, "It appears we have some time before they try anything. That allows us to negotiate a solution."

Butler huffed.

"In the meantime, we need to get that base going, Bo," he turned to Butler, "have you made any progress on it?"

"On Sharia? Yeah, I've spoken with their leaders, and they are willing to go ahead with the base." Beau paused for a moment, "Of course, they want some compensation for allowing it."

"Compensation? Protection from the Kazons should be enough." Pencaster said.

"You'd think," Richerson agreed.

"And the division for Kryth?" Pencaster asked Butler.

"In progress and operational in another two weeks."

"How long will it take to get the base established?" Richerson asked.

"I'll have a workable start in three months, eight to have it fully manned."

"I'll bring Wilson up to date," Pencaster said.

"Now, about the Kazons," Richerson turned to Bove and Stella, "we'll take them into custody. Bo, will you see to that?"

Butler said, "Right away. Then to Bove, "Take me to them."

*        *        *

Back on the Ibex after Butler had taken the Kazons, Bove, and Stella joined the crew on the bridge. "Did the others make it off okay?" Bove asked Jack.

"Once again, good riddance to Tom," Jack stated.

"Yeah," Lucy added.

"Agreed," Stella said.

Dan glared at her and shrugged his shoulders.

"And the others?" Bove asked.

"Yeah, they were glad to be home. Steve said he hadn't seen his family in two years. Mike said it was a year for him, and Raymond said he still had to get home, someplace in South America."

"We could have dropped him there."

"He didn't want to impose," Jack said.

"I guess we need to get you home," Bove said to Stella.

"Yeah?" She lowered her head and glanced up at Bove.

"We'll miss you, "Jack added.

"Yeah," Lucy said. "I'll miss having a companion. If you haven't noticed, I'm the only female on board. It gets tiresome."

"I'm sure," Stella said and smiled at Bove. "You know," she looked around the bridge at each console, "It seems you're a crew member short," she nodded toward Tom's seat. "And," she added, "with all that cargo I would think you should have someone to manage it."

"Are you asking for a job?" Bove looked into her eyes hopefully.

"Are you offering?"

"Yes," Lucy said over Bove, then glanced at Bove unsure if she had overstepped or not.

Bove nodded at Lucy, "There you have it," he turned to Stella. "Welcome our new cargo manager." He smiled and she smiled back with sparkling eyes.

"Where to," Ryan asked firing up the engines.

"We have a cargo bay full of cesium that needs a buyer," Bove tapped the arm of his captain's chair.

"Well," Dan turned from his console, "I know a guy."

Old people are the future you.

Acknowledgments

Thanks to my brother Dion for his suggestions to improve the manuscript. Thanks to Lorin Oberwager for her critique and valuable insights into the story. And to White Dog Publishing.

# About the author

Jon H. Costales writes science fiction and fantasy novels. He is the author of The Adventures of Bove Sandle series which includes Visions of Redemption. He lives with his wife in a suburb south of Atlanta, Georgia with pet cats, a dog, and a turtle. For the latest about works in progress see Jon's website at: www.joncostaleswriter.com